I0534986

A Book of Fiction

Joe A. Melendez

Just Ruthless

Joe A. Melendez

Joe A. Melendez

Introduction

Hi, my name is Johnny Redbone and I'm about to tell you the true story about Adam Stockton and Chris Gomez, the two stars of "Just Ruthless". The last time Adam and Chris were in the public eye, they were uncharacteristically deceitful. The truth is that these two scumbags actually helped me get out of a pretty bad mess and in doing so they paid with their honor and pride. So now I feel a bit obligated to get the straight story out into the public. The things that I'm about to tell you I know because of my personal involvement in the story, some of it was told to me by Adam and Chris, and other things I saw on the show, like most people. I'll try not to bullshit you as much as possible.

But please bear with me, I live a very interesting life and as a result my memory tends to fade in and out.

Adam and Chris's story starts with the idea of a very shrewd and determined television producer by the name of Pierre Nadaju. Mr. Nadaju was a short, middle-aged man with a slender build. He wore rimless, oval glasses and would sport a wonderfully awful comb-over. He was a reality show genius, not that it really takes one to think of them; but he was really good at finding the perfect product to sell. With every hit show, he made fortunes for several men, himself included. By this point in his career, he pretty much had the power and the money to do whatever he wanted, but "Just Ruthless" would be his greatest project ever.

It would become a global phenomenon. Television would make Adam and Chris huge stars in the United States, but with the help of the internet, their debauchery and childish antics would made them the biggest stars in the world. The "Just Ruthless" phenomenon spread quickly and the results were pretty fucking ridiculous and silly especially once you know the truth.

The Rat Race

Pierre Nadaju walks around an empty office building. He begins to speak softly as he looks straight into the camera. "Several months ago, this network and its affiliates decided to purchase an already existing software development company called Hardmega Technology. We did very little to change the structure of the business. We merely cleaned the place up and stuck cameras in just about every possible inch of the building. The office is located in this corporate office building, here in downtown Manhattan, New York City, the greatest and most diverse city in the entire universe.

This show (*Nadaju pauses for dramatic effect*) is about diversity and how people react with each other in real situations. Camera crews will not be following the people that you will be seeing on the show, but we will always be keeping an eye on them. Ladies and gentlemen, we now bring you "The Rat Race".

The intro music begins to play. It's a pop song performed by a famous pop-singer. Hopefully the association between commercial success and something brand new would be obvious to the public. The music played while a short montage video, with footage from the different cameras in the offices, was shown. The music ends and the camera pans to Pierre Nadaju standing by a cubicle holding his hands together, as if to show eagerness in anticipation for something. He begins to speak and releases his hands.

"The people that you will meet and see through out these cubicles are regular folk; they didn't have to audition for this job, aside from the initial interview that was given to them when applying for their positions. They are here to work, to make money to support lives and families, not to become famous or to win a huge cash sum. In fact, they won't even know when they are being filmed. These people that you will all meet have no clue at all that our cameras are there. We will be bringing to you the different stories and lives that exist in the stressful world of that which we like to call "The Rat Race". And the cameras go off.

Relax, we'll get to the whole "Just Ruthless" bullshit, but the story starts with another reality show called "The Rat Race". You didn't think "Just Ruthless" would be an original show did you? Like anything else in life, it too is another shitty spin-off of something just as bad.

So, back to the show.

First of all, most of what Nadaju said was bullshit. The people working at Hardmega Technology were told about the reality show, they signed a clause that would force them to act completely oblivious that the show even existed. They went through an orientation. They sat in a room. They were prodded, I'm sure.

The truth is that most people are actually pretty boring unless you tell them that they might be on television. Therefore Mr. Nadaju felt that it would make a more authentic and exciting reality show if people weren't so realistic and average.

Pierre is an asshole. There is only so long that I can stomach him for; so, for my own personal satisfaction and not at all to appease any of you who might be reading this, I'd like to tell you about Adam Stockton.

Adam Stockton

This young man with a very good heart was unfortunately stricken with the inability to keep his mouth shut, especially during more awkward and inappropriate moments. His name is Adam Stockton. He is an average looking guy with average hair, average teeth and average clothes. He went to an average university where he partied hard and got average grades. He got an average degree in computer science and quickly found himself an average job with Hardmega Technology, almost as soon as he graduated. In the eyes of most humans, Adam Stockton was nothing more than an average man in his early twenties.

Adam Stockton saw the world, as it was seen by most, as he rode the subway on this Monday morning. He saw nothing out of the ordinary. He had seen the same faces everyday staring back at him with little contentment. The pudgy short guy with the unfitting shirt and the unhealthy pasty white, sweaty complexion always sat next to the little Asian lady with the black PBS bag. No matter how crowded the train was or what season it might be, these two looked the same. Different color shirts and PBS bags altered the appearance of the two from time to time. Regardless, the sweat stains and grim faces always stayed the same.

Adam didn't bother looking around the train much. There were times when a young couple, still enjoying their night out on the town and very much enjoying each other, would distract him from studying "Piggy" and "Contribution ". Those were the nicknames he had given to the two very inanimate individuals.

He never had spoken to any of the two directly, he did, however, nod hello to both of them from time to time.

The train stopped, and the doors slid open, this was his final destination. It might as well have been his ultimate destination. Adam hated his job. He had one of "those" jobs, with much emphasis on the "those" aspect of it. He sat in a cubicle with three and a quarter walls, two inches thick, four feet tall and made of some highly flammable, highly economical, state-of-the-art, space age material…

Plastic.

He drank coffee with lots of sugar and no milk, listened to Black Sabbath on his portable MP3 player and picked his nose with the same finger that he used to stir the sugar in his coffee. If you need to ask me "What Adam actually did for a living?", than you aren't paying close enough attention. He worked with computers, asshole. And he did what most people probably do all day long at work. That would be staring at a screen and clicking on his mouse.

He had gotten his routine down to a science. Here, let me turn on the show for a while, so you can observe for yourself.

Back to the Show

Adam Stockton sat at his desk, staring into a mug full of steaming coffee. He opened a packet, poured some sugar, repeated this three to six times, picked his nose with right hand index finger, flicked it, stirred his coffee with same finger, hummed "War Pigs", took a sip, and click............click.........click.

He did this shit for eight hours a day, five days a week, 49 weeks a year, for $45,000 dollars gross annual income that paid for a small apartment, nicely decorated, and no car. There weren't too many complaints coming from Adam about the "situation" that he lived with.

"Shit, people are dying on the streets of Bombay." Adam would say, despite the fact that he had never actually been to Bombay, or seen any actual photos of the current state of Bombay. But I think we can all safely agree with him that it must be a shithole.

Click....click......Backspace.....delete....click.....print.....

"What's going on Adam?"

That's Jim or John, maybe Jacob. He's that guy in the office that you see and talk to just about every day, but only when he approaches you, because you never remember his name.

"Hey, um....guy. What's up?" Adam didn't want to ask, but felt it necessary.

Jim or John, maybe Jacob isn't necessarily a bad guy. He's just too comfortable when it comes to touching people, but not in a sexual way. He just tends to put his arm around your shoulders and squeeze and push you.

"So, have you seen the new girl in personnel?" Jim or John, maybe Jacob whispered in Adam's ear as he fumbled through Adam's hair followed by a yank. Adam could only compare this to his days as an altar boy helping out, Father McSpankin. Luckily, Adam had all those memories mostly blocked out.

Thank God.

"Ah...Yeah, she's pretty hot. The blonde right?" Adam could have kicked himself in the face for asking a question and giving Jim or John, maybe Jacob a reason to stick around.

"Yeah the Blonde, blah blah blah. Did you see her blah...." He's even too boring for me to transcribe.

"Yeah she's hot, real go-getter-looker-slut with a nice smile, beautiful." Adam couldn't concentrate past the fact that it felt as if it were well over two hundred degrees in the office while this nameless baboon with a big heart and bigger balls, but no common decency, just couldn't keep his paws to himself.

"Hey, sorry to have to cut this short," Not short enough if you asked Adam "but I have to finish up with this thing that I was doing before you came here. I don't mean to say that I don't want to talk to you right now. You just have to understand that I'm doing this by special request from the Assistant VP of packaging. It's big "hush-hush" top secret, no bullshit stuff. So, I need to get back to this before one of the higher ups puts my stick in his ass. I mean my ass on a stick or a stick up my ass. You understand, right?"

"Hey man. Yeah, yeah I know what you mean. Just last week," When John or Bill or Jonathan, whatever-his-name-is latches on, there is no getting free, "I was handed this report....."

Oh how Adam wished he was back with Father McSpankin for a minute. At least then it was just a physical thing.

"That's great." Said Adam followed by some "No shit."

Click...Click...

He figured maybe if he showed that he was actually busy solving the perils of the dark realm of packaging by clicking on a deck of virtual solitaire, maybe, just maybe, Ronald or Jim maybe Jacob would get the hint to vamoose. He was wrong.

"....so then I was like, 'Man, I swear to God if you keep touching my'. Oh shit. There she is." What's-his-name had kept talking.

"Who?" Adam cursed the evil genius that created such a monstrous card game, never even noticed the tall blonde slinking by.

"Dude, the fucking blonde from personnel!" Jimbo Von Nudendyke proclaimed eagerly. How's that for a name?

"Oh yeah man she's a piece of ass, you should get on the prowl and totally hunt her down, killer."

"Yeah, yeah here I go. Wish me luck."

"All right there chieftain, fuck off." Adam mumbled as he brushed this dude's paw away his shoulder with his hand.

"Hey man, thanks." Mr. Nameless said as Adam ignored him.

Click taka taka taka click taka taka click......

That exchange made Adam thirst for a cigarette. So he decided to step outside for a second. The walk down the corridor of death was pretty bad for the simple fact that any person over the height of three feet eleven inches could not hide behind the sanctuary of the mighty cubicle barracks. Adam would use the "sick" trick to try to avoid everyone. He would place his hand over his mouth as if he needed to upchuck and then take long sloppy strides all the way to the elevator. When the elevator opens, sometimes the sight of a sick looking person that seemed ready to explode would be enough to evacuate it. This time Adam stopped his acting before the elevator arrived.

"God damn yuppie laws, can't even smoke in buildings." He said as he entered the empty elevator. He hit the button for the ground floor and looked ahead. The elevator stopped and opened on the eighth floor, in walked in a fine specimen of the large North American female human species. It can be understandable how there can be certain people who have some form of eating disorder or glandular problem. However, what boggled Adam was the total lack of acknowledgment of appropriate attire for a woman of such pseudo-voluptuous assets.

"Lycra spandex really holds it in." Adam thought out loud, a little bit too loud at that.

"What did you say?" Strangely, questioned the large woman.

"Those damn surgeons really botched the operation."

"What the fuck does that mean?!" The rhino had become angry.

"No sorry, the surgeons who worked on my eyes made things look larger than they really are." It's a little known fact that giving people crazy sounding answers can make you seem crazy and most people don't like continuing crazy conversations with crazy people that they still have not gotten to know on a personal or professional level.

Needless to say, the next seven-floor descent was awkward

Ping!

Doors opened.

"Generals gather in the masses," Adam sang in a weak Ozzy voice. "Hey Duke!"

Adam yelled as he spotted the security guard Lavash, his African American work related associate.

"Yo, What Up bro?" Lavash was a horse of a man. God had removed Lavash's neck area and had replaced it with a boulder. God had also put a little girl's voice box inside that giant boulder. "Brother, you smoke too much cigarettes." The man was solid as a rock, even inside his head.

"Well you big John Henry motherfucker, cancer affects only those who are scared of getting cancer."

"Well you're getting emphysema and birth defects." Lavash said this with much enthusiasm, as if he had just knocked out Mike Tyson, whom happens to be his physical and verbal counterpart.

Smoking cigarettes was always an interesting part of the day for Adam. He could just stand outside; stare at the people walking by as they were dreading their very existences in this corporate universe.

"Yo Lavash. What's the deal with toupees?" Asked Adam.

"That Nigga got shot by Biggie's boys." Lavash answered.

"No not Tupac. Toupees. Like hair pieces, you know, for bald guys?" Adam hoped that he knew

"Man, beats me. It just looks like some dead ass frog on some bald dude's head"

"You mean cat."

"Nah bro, not the cat, the fucking dude over there with the rug."

Adam stared at Lavash in disbelief. "You work out too much, man. You shouldn't strain yourself so much. You seem to be bursting too many essential neurons."

In the midst of stepping back to let a crowd pass by, Adam stepped down on someone. "Oh shit, I'm sorry." He said as he turned around to see whose toes he just crushed.

Gawk.

Adam had stepped right on the foot of the blonde girl from personnel. "No really I'm sorry. I'll buy you some shoes."

(She laughs) "You're going to buy me some shoes?" said the Blonde, with more grace and sexual spillage then a nuclear meltdown in a raunchy French brothel.

Adam just shrugged because he just didn't really have any thoughts in his head, except for one. That one thought was *"why can't I think?"*

"You're going to have to take me shoe shopping." She said with a smile.

"OK." Adam's brain had just burst or maybe it was a testicle or his wallet. "Wait, what?" He asked.

"You said you'd buy me shoes. So, you have to take me shopping for shoes. It's your duty as a gentleman and man of honor."

"Yo, I'm not from Georgia, but my father once told me 'Son, if a pretty lady ever asks you to take her somewhere, you take her and show her the time of her life.'"

"That's so sweet. Your dad sounds like a very nice guy."

"He's dead."

"Oh, I'm sorry. I didn't know. I...."

Adam interrupts her, "Don't worry its okay. You didn't kill him."

The blonde let out an awkward laugh. It was a noise that came from the dimension placed somewhere between laughter and a scream for help.

"Don't laugh. I killed the fucker." Adam made sure to say this in an extremely believable way. "Hey I'm just messing with you. I just say very stupid things when I get nervous."

"I'm sorry to have made you nervous. That definitely wasn't my intention. I was just trying to be friendly."

Now Adam was extremely confused. The noise in his head came from a universe stuck somewhere between the dimension where the sounds made by males like Lavash getting kicked straight in the testicles came from and the dimension where alligators are fed to chickens, just to produce sounds for Adam's head. I swear to you all that this is exactly how Adam explained it to me.

"So were you being friendly just to be nice or friendly so I can take you shoe shopping?" He continued clumsily.

"Well perhaps a little of both; but I tell you what. How about we postpone the shoe-shopping thing for a later date? How about you just take me to a movie or something?"

"Did I step on your movie too?"

"Still nervous?"

"No, just really stupid." Adam thought to himself about just how stupid he was being. He figured that one was only as stupid as one thinks he is. Unless, you are too stupid to realize that you are actually dumber then you think you are, therefore making yourself out to be smarter then you should know that you aren't. He is a true a philosopher.

"But, I'm not stupid enough to let down a prime opportunity like this slip away. So, how about you and I go see a feature flick down at the adult theater; or you can pick the place and the movie."

"You're weird."

"Yeah, but you like it."

She giggled like a little schoolgirl, whom was just passed a note from her little crush sitting across the schoolroom. "Ok, here's my number. Call me after work and we'll make plans."

"You got it, beautiful." Adam was feeling pretty damn good as he watched her walk away down the sidewalk.

He lit up another cigarette. He smoked half of it enthusiastically, put it out and went back to his cubicle with a lot more confidence. This time he made sure everyone in their designated cubicles, which he passed by on his way to his own, noticed him. He whistled out loud, tapped on the top of dividers, high-fived the mailroom guy (who we'll meet soon), and did the ol' "click, click" sound with his tongue as he fired his index finger at the secretaries. Finally, Adam was back at his chair, after his victory lap.

The little red light on his telephone was blinking, which indicated that he had received a message. "God damn it", he thought. A message only meant more work for Adam.

"Hey, umm..Adam....Yeah....This is Walter Maxwell from purchasing.....um...I wanted to know, well I was told that I needed to call you if I ever needed some copier paper for my fax machine......Thanks....um....my extension is 8743."

No more messages.

Adam hangs up and dials Mr. Walter Maxwell's extension. It's ringing......still ringing.....ringing still...."Hello you have reached the desk of Walter Maxwell. I'm sorry that I can not be of any help right now, but please leave your name and extension and I'll get back to you as soon as possible......beep."

"Yeah Hi....um....Walter. This is Adam Stockton over at quality assurance. I have your copier paper and if you would like to ever see it again, place three thousand dollars in small-unmarked bills in an inter-office envelope. Mail it over and I'll contact you. Thank you."

"Sup bro, you've got a package." Chris, the mailroom guy, stepped into the picture. I told you we would meet him soon. This is Chris Gomez; he is the one responsible for telling people to call Adam's extension if they needed copier paper.

"I hope it's not a bomb.....Hahahaha." Adam is a regular Seinfeld.

"Yeah man. It's a fucking bomb or maybe a human head. No, better yet, it has anthrax in it." Chris didn't seem too amused about

Adam's delightful and seemingly harmless remark. "Yeah, I know you think it's very delightful and seemingly harmless to joke about their being a bomb in your package. But, you know what? It gets boring quickly. I've heard bomb three times today, anthrax eight times, human head three, and some ingenious dude asked, 'Is it a baby fetus?'

That was actually pretty funny, though. But, just..." This story occurred shortly after the terrorist attacks that destroyed the World Trade Center in lower Manhattan.

There was a slight pause as Chris took a deep breath, "Look, they don't pay me enough to deliver stupid, retarded items that all you stupid computer punching geeks keep fucking ordering from e-bay, because all of your jobs are so pointless and boring, that the only thing in the world to bring a little pleasure to your miserable careers and lives is ordering junk from the internet. God damn it."

"Well...um...Chris. I am very sorry for joking about such a terrible subject. I know it's stupid, but.."

"Dude no. Man I just needed to vent on somebody. You know. I have no money, my life is lame and my boss sucks. I just vented on you because I know that you're a bigger scumbag than I am, so you probably deserved it. Plus, you seem like you can take a joke or a shit fit like that and not bug out."

Sometimes, people actually see things in the same way. It creates a sense of unity. Once in a while, people actually can share the experience by seeing the world how it actually is, together, and not how most people perceive it to be, alone. This brought some clarity into Adam's deranged mind.

"You're right, Chris. You're fucking right. This fucking job sucks, my career sucks, and my pay sucks. I don't even know who my boss is really. I fucking HATE THIS FUCKING PLACE!"

Chris's face took on a more confused look then Adam's had. "Yeah man. Right on. Fucking....Give 'em hell man. Go get 'em. So..... Can you just sign right here? No not there. Over here. Where it's highlighted. Yeah. Alright man. Have a good one. I gotta go finish this, so I can go veg out. Peace."

"Later man. Take care." Adam's moment of rage ended as soon as he forgot what he was pissed off about.

"Oh look, box!" Adam thought as he looked down at his desk. He took out his Swiss Army knife and pulled out the blade from it. He used it to slice the packing tape on the box and looked inside. "Oh My god!" Adam couldn't believe his eyes. Inside that box was it. It was what every man has always wanted and will always want. Now Adam had one of them and his quest for it was finally over. He couldn't believe his eyes, his mind, even his heart felt a sense of deception. His stomach was turning, and his head was spinning with excitement. The only thing that stood in his way for eternal bliss was just one more layer of wrapping. The suspense was killing him. "God damn fucking mutant wrapping, I'm so close." Adam thought.

There it was. There was Adam's Holy Grail. His last breathe of air, his heart's last beat, the key to all the love and happiness that he shall ever need and want, his….

"Fuck! Wrong color."

There really was no point in keeping it, for Adam, if it wasn't the right color that he wanted. Satisfaction is a key point to happiness. How could he be happy unless he's content and satisfied, and this right here was not making Adam happy?

He wrapped it up, taped the box back up, affixed the return sticker, and placed it by the outgoing mail. It came with good intentions and all the blissfulness in the world. It had lit up Adam's life with sheer excitement, but it wasn't right. It wasn't right for him. Somewhere out there was a man in a cubicle that likes it in that color and hopefully, one day maybe, he will be united with it.

"Yo Susan."

Susan was Adam's co-worker, female advisor, therapist, biggest critic and vent for all his bitching and ranting that he constantly had to release.

"Susan."

"What's going on man?" She peered over the wall of the cubicle. Susan was a very perplexing female specimen. Physically, she was very deceiving.

One day, she seemed like just another plain looking woman in her mid-twenties, in a pantsuit, with her hair up in a bun, wearing those square frame glasses that are very popular amongst the intellectual hipsters hanging around your local coffee shops. Then some other days, she was this hot chick, especially on casual Fridays. She'd have on some really tight pants, hair loose and a revealing shirt, all tasteful and not too slutty. Maybe it was the fact that it showed off her perfect body, or that Adam was basically always horny, but it made him want to "hit that".

"Hey, I got it today."

"No shit, let me see it." Susan peered over with much excitement.

"Oh, you can't; I sent it back."

"What? Why?" Susan couldn't believe that any man would want to get rid of it.

"It wasn't the right color. Those fucking people over in that company don't know how to get it right. It's always one thing or another. I can never get it."

"Man that blows. Yeah they seem to always fuck it up." Susan said as she nodded her head in disappointment.

Susan is a cool chick which makes her even more attractive.

"It can never be done right, ever. I bet I'm still going to end up paying for it. It always comes back to bite me in the ass, always. It's so ridiculous. It's un-American. That's what it is. They should have a law against it.

You know?

If they promise you it one way, then you should get it that way, the way that it was supposed to and meant to be.

Anyways, I got a date with that hot blonde from personnel." Susan received a wink and a smile from Adam, as his mood just so drastically changed.

"With the boobs?"

"Yeah, they'll be there too." Another wink and smile from Adam.

"Where are you guys going?"

"I think we're going to do the whole "movie and a dinner" thing."

"I think that's dinner and a movie."

"Nope, it's movie first, then dinner. If I go eat dinner first, I'm going to get full and maybe drink something or two. Then I'll be all tired and sleepy during the movie. I don't want to fall asleep on our first date. Plus, if we go to a movie first, then she'll get full on popcorn and not want to go out to dinner and if she still did, she probably wouldn't order as much."

"Wow. That's some pretty good logic. But, how about you don't eat so much and maybe, just maybe, you don't get drunk." Hand it to a woman to speak with common sense.

"You have no idea what you're talking about. You women never get it, do you?"

"Why do you even talk to me? You never have anything good to say." Susan replied.

"Hey, you want to come with us on our date? We can make it a threesome night. We can even skip the movie." Adam really did wish that in this universe in which he lived that this would actually be possible and happen.

"Oh yeah? Is that a promise? Maybe I can bring some of my hot lesbians friends with me too."

"Just make sure they're clean. I don't want any dirty hoes. Haha." Adam had now regressed into a giddy little thirteen year old boy.

"Douche bag. Grow up." And she disappeared behind her cubicle wall.

Adam got up and peeked over. "I love you."

"Asshole." She replied satisfactorily as Adam submerged into his chair.

Click....Click.......drag, paste, select, delete, print, grab sheet, get up, go make some copies.

Having to use the copy machine was never a fun activity for Adam. The damned machine was always jammed or out of toner, and no one else was smart enough to fix it. Using it also left Adam opened to the general public for shitty conversation from shitty co-workers.

"Oh hey, David. What's up?" Adam could curse himself for initially making eye contact with this man, thus forcing him to say hello first.

"Oh hey, Adam. I didn't see you there."

"Oh yeah? I can never tell." He hadn't seen Adam. Now, Adam was really cursing himself and David. How was it David's fault? Well it's not David's "fault" so-to-say. It's more like God's or David's crack head mother's fault. David is badly cross-eyed. You could never tell when he was looking at you. Sometimes, when he seemed to be looking at you, he really was not. Therefore, logic would have it, that when he didn't seem to be looking at you, he really was, but not always. This is why Adam couldn't figure him out. "So how's it going? What's going on at the ol' homestead? Duke." At least he's trying to be polite in his demented little way. Listen, give him a break. This is hard for Adam.

"Well, you know Adam, there has been a surge in the decrease of mutual bond rates in the recent quarter. You should look deeply into it within the next week or two. Bababababababababababababababababababababababababababababababababababababa ba…"

Adam might as well have been hit with a frying pan from the hands of Bugs Bunny in Toon Town. He had a look that stood somewhere between "Hey your dog just died." And "Fuck. I didn't pull out on time." At times like this, Adam's mind was so deeply in shock, that lying didn't work. Lying would require innovation. Innovation was usually the first thing to be thrown out of Adam's brain when something confused him at this level.

"What the fuck are you talking about? What mutual bond? What quarter? Who are you looking at? Were you talking to me?" Adam still stood in shock, but he would not be the only one now.

"Hey man, sorry. Shit. I was just trying to be a nice fucking guy and hinting you in to some good financial advice. I know how you young guys always need more money."

Adam thought about how David was probably only a year or two older then him.

"What? What are you talking about? You're not that much older then me. You're either burnt or you should be. Watch out. I've got some copies to make." Adam couldn't bear to be around anal-retentive people.

"Great, the copy machine is broken again." Adam mumbled.

Now he had to go to the other side of the room, all the way on the other side of the office, where all the really annoying people sat.

"Just fly on through, man. You can get through this. No problem." Adam chanted to himself while he whisked through the extremely tight hallway between the cubicles.

"Adam!"

"Fuck." Adam was about to encounter the worst of them all. Claradette is somewhere between thirty-five to sixty-two years old. She looks a little bit like a troll, only a little bit taller; unless trolls are really tall. She has been in serious need of a hair styling makeover fiasco ages ago. Her hair goes from red straw-like material looking at the tips, to orange, then yellowish, finally gray and white at the roots. Stocky. Oddly enough, those seemed to be her only good qualities. If David was anal retentive, Claradette was born without an asshole.

"Hey Adam, you see this?" She was pointing at some report he had done earlier.

"No, what are you talking about?"

"You see the staple here?" She really was building up to climax now.

"Yeah, so what?" Adam really did hope she needed to crawl back under whatever bridge she had lived in.

"It's too close to the top of the report. If someone where to turn one of the pages a little too hard, it might rip right off. See." She demonstrated.

Try it at home for yourselves. It'll only take a moment. You don't even have to pause this. Just put the book down. I'll wait.

Stop being lazy.

Do it.

Okay, thank you. Let's continue.

"The copy machine did the stapling. Sometimes it doesn't fall quite exactly right unto the tray. So what?" Adam was very excited to hear what she had to say.

"Well, you know that one of the V.P.'s may get a little ticked off if one of the pages accidentally flies out of the booklet."

"I tell you what Clarinet, if one of them has any complaints about the booklets, you bring them to me. Okay?"

"Um...ok. Fine, but just remember I'm not going to be the one in trouble. If one of those guys disapproves about the booklets, I'm going to make sure I tell them that it wasn't my fault, but yours."

"Fuck off." Adam murmured under his breath and dazed off as she continued her babbling....

Pay Attention

Adam daydreamed often, even more so than your average normal scumbag. He would bore easily and his avid imagination helped overcome the effects associated with having to listen to boring assholes all the time. His imagination might have helped him keep his sanity at many different times in his life, but there was a time that it came to bite him in the ass, hard, really fucking hard. A couple of months earlier, Hardmega Tech had been acquired by some big corporation that does what corporations do. Adam didn't care. He would make more money and that is always nice. So.

A couple of weeks ago, Adam had to attend a meeting, one of those real big "must attend" meetings. It was being led by some guy, wearing some shitty suit with some psychedelic tie. I can see how a person more in touch with reality could get a real kick out of a tie like that. This man, however, wore that tie because of his lack of fashion and lack of interest towards anything truly important on this earth, like getting laid. Adam figured that a person not interested in sex, in any shape or form, couldn't possibly be a human.

So there was Adam, sitting three rows back from the front, listening to this man ramble about some very important shit. But as the man went on, Adam couldn't stop staring at his tie. If Adam actually paid attention to the meeting, he would have learned some very crucial information, information that could change his life and the output of this story. Luckily for us, he paid absolutely no attention during the Rat Race reality show orientation, instead he daydreamt.

"This man must be an alien." He thought.

Adam's mind wandered. He tried to figure out more details about the tie by staring at it fierce-fully, the color scheme of that tie could not be found anywhere else. The first time Adam remembered seeing colors like those was in a National Geographic issue that had some pictures from the Hubble telescope. The last time was after taking all some acid back in college.

This man's tie looked like one of those nebulas located thirty-five billion light years from here. So it was simply a matter of deductive reasoning for Adam. That tie was not from this earth. That man must have gotten it on a different planet. We earthlings do not have the technology for long-range space travel. Thus, this man must be a space alien.

Adam stared at this creature's tie for the first half hour of the meeting. He was locked in. Wherever this man would move, Adam's eyes would follow the tie. Soon, the colors were engulfing everything. They first spread out unto the man's suit; not even Jesus could have had a more Technicolor suit then this one. Then it radiated unto the projection screen, where this space alien had been transmitting weird celestial voodoo images from a laptop hooked up to a digital projector.

That must have been alien technology as well.

The colors then started going up the wall, up unto the ceiling, and down the wall, down unto the floor. It was spreading fast, real fast. Adam started to get excited but not scared. If anything, he was merely, very intrigued. He thought about how there was probably no better way to die than by being engulfed by a weird alien, killer tie. Soon, the whole room was painted with this color scheme. But this too got boring for Adam after a quick minute, until the colors and walls and this strange space-alien-financial-consultant started to undulate and melt, then resurface from the puddle.

"Stop giggling." Susan kept telling him, as she poked into his ribs with her elbow. Susan had daydreamt herself, but she dreamt of going to Hollywood and making television shows. She told Adam, who in turn then told me, about how she could never understand why he never mentioned the television show or show any interest in it. She figured he was sticking to the clause, which was being discussed earlier in the meeting.

Eventually, it was over. Everyone stood up wearing mixed faces and glistening eyes. They were all told to come up to the front of the conference room and sign a contract. Adam merely followed Susan and did as she did but he stopped for a second and Adam went over to the space alien and shook his hand. "I have never met such a great speaker before. By the way, where did you get that tie?"

"It was a gift from mother." The alien replied in a very serious way, a little too serious for Adam. Was he speaking in code? Who really was "mother" and where did she get that tie? All very interesting questions that Adam would soon forget once he had gotten back to his cubicle.

Regardless of the actual truth, Adam never realized he had just agreed to be part of a reality show to be filmed in his office.

You Suck

Clueless, Adam stared down at this troll, Claradette. He started to wonder how anyone could take anything so stupid and boring like this job so serious. He pictured her going home to a smoky house, full of smoky cats and her ancient parents still alive, still bitching, still controlling her every thought. He figured that this pitiful job was her only outlet to the outside world.

She won some shitty celebrity reality show recently. She's still scary looking.

"Has she ever been laid?" Adam thought, "That would be a horrible thing." He no longer hated her or was disgusted by her, well, perhaps a little physically. Adam had a plan. He figured all he had to do was get this lady laid. The problem was going to be finding someone willing enough to do this heinous deed. I'll tell you right now and spare you any disappointment. Adam totally forgets about her by the next chapter and you will too, probably.

"Clarinet, don't worry about it. I'll see to it that you get satisfied." He said as she walked away.

Adam had totally forgotten why he was standing up now. But remembered as he looked down to see what was in his hand. "That's right!" He thought. "Must make copies."

This time, Adam headed for the copy machine with his head pointing straight down. He wasn't going to take another chance at eye contact with anyone else.

"Fuck!" Adam wondered whether he said that a little too loud.

The copy machine had a sign on it that said "Jammed and Out of Toner, Called in for Repairs, Thank You". Adam remembered when his refrigerator broke; he needed to call someone to come for it to be repaired. He knew he needed to call it in for repairs, because he doesn't even know how a refrigerator works. Maybe, if it had a little screen on the front of it that told you just how to fix and repair the appliance by showing you little animated pictures, then maybe he would have been able to repair it without the assistance of a trained professional.

Now, as for the copy machine, it tells you what to do right on its little menu screen. *Open door one, pull down section two, pull out tray three, remove jammed paper. Close tray three, pull up section two, close door one. Wait as copier warms up. Add black toner.* Then, there is a little cartoon on the display showing you step by step how to add the toner. Adam was able to fix it after five minutes of tampering with it. He finished just in time for the copy repair guy to look at it.

"Too late dude, I fixed it." Normally someone who had just accomplished such a feat would have a look of satisfaction and pride in their eyes, but Adam knew exactly what the copier repair guy was thinking.

"Why do you people waste my time? If you knew you could fix it, then why did you call it in?" The look of annoyance on the face of this pale thin man could not be mistaken for anything else but that, annoyance.

"Hey dude, I didn't call it in. I just came over to make some copies and it had a note on it saying that it was jammed and it needed toner, so I fixed it. The secretary must have put that note or maybe one of these other morons in here did it. But, it wasn't me." Adam needed to make it quite clear that he was not the douche bag responsible for this man's time being wasted. Adam believes in the philosophy of live and let live. You don't fuck with him; he won't fuck with you.

"Ok, but you tell all these morons in here to only call me if the god damn copier blows up or threatens to kill everyone. Alright?" He just got a hint of color in his cheeks as he made sure he made his point understandable.

"Okay." Adam felt that there was no real use in continuing this conversation with this hostile and disturbed individual. He finally made his copies, even though the machine jammed several times in the process. Adam then walked over to the secretary's desk.

"Did you put that sign on the copy machine?" Adam asked the secretary, Janis Robinson.

"Yes I did. It was jammed and needed toner." Janis was from some West Indian nation. Adam guessed this because of her accent and the fact that she was always complaining about being cold, never mind the fact that the thermostat was on eighty-five degrees and she was sweating profusely. She had long blonde extensions in her hair and was easily pushing four hundred pounds. Adam was somewhat intimidated by her style and overall look; however, he hated her too much to let such a petty thing like fear stand in his way to tell her off.

"Why didn't you un-jam it and add toner yourself?" Adam took a step back just to be on the safe side.

"Because dat is not my jub. Plus I don't know how to do it myself."

"What the hell is your job? I never see you doing anything. You just sit there talking to your girlfriends on the phone. I shouldn't even have to be making my own copies, for Christ's sake. You know I'm really busy," Adam needed to add some bullshit in the mix in order to make himself seem important. Adam NEVER had too much work to do. "Regardless, how do you NOT know how to do it? It tells you how. Right there," Adam pointed and shook his finger at the machine, "It's fool proof. Any dumbass can do it. Shit, it isn't my job to do it either, but I still figured it out."

"Ju listen to me, OK. Ju don't talk to me wit dat tone of voice. I know what my jub is and I know how to do it. I don't get up and go over to you cubicle and tell you what you do and don't do." Adam took another step back fearing that she would strike at him like a hippo in a pond full of giant marbles.

"First of all, you never get up. I don't think you even go home or use the bathroom or anything, because it would involve exertion. Secondly, you don't do anything and you get paid for it, so don't complain. The least you can do is make sure the copy machine is functional." Adam fumbled for a piece of candy that he might have had in his pocket. He figured it might distract her for a second if she lunged at him, giving him enough time to run for it.

He then remembered something he heard on the discovery channel about how hippos can sprint up to thirty miles an hour. But, that might have been rhinos; nevertheless, he wasn't going to take the chance with this beast. So, before she could retaliate, he dashed back to his cubicle with the copies he had just made. He made it back in twenty-six seconds flat. He beat his previous record by three seconds.

"Oh look." Adam saw that the little red light on his telephone was blinking again. "Message," he thought. Then, he thought some more. He wondered whether it was a good idea to pick up the phone or just let it be. He could deal working at a desk with a blinking red light. It might actually make his area a little more exciting and daring, like a miniature party strobe light. "Yeah, that's it." Adam thought. "A party on my desk where I'm the only one invited. I'll be the coolest guy in the office."

So there was Adam, sitting contently at his desk, staring at the little red flashing party strobe light embedded in his telephone. He could hear the gay club music playing at first, but then he decided that this was his party and he was going to be the one to select the music. "Fishbone, yeah," He thought as he mentally praised himself for such a great choice in musical selection, "Fishbone is red hot!" (For those of you not familiar with the afro-punk/ska/funk/jazz band from Los Angeles, California, you should become more familiar with them.)

He continued to stare at the light. More and more he became entranced by the blinking effect. Deeper and deeper he stared into it. Until, finally, it shot at him. Like the Death Star laser beam, but it didn't hit him directly. It blew past him, just whizzing past his ear.

Now, Adam was interested. The beam continued to whiz past him, over and over again, flying past his head with incredible speed.

"Ohohohoohoooha...." He kept making a weird sound, as if he were receiving the best blowjob of his life.

"Yo, Adam." Chris, the mailroom guy, had been looking at Adam stare at the red light for about five minutes now, "Wake the fuck up."

"The world that is portrayed may not be the one that it appears to be. It may also not be the one that you think it is. So possibly, by seeing the world through the eyes of someone else who you think is not the viewer of the current world, you may actually get a clearer picture." Mr. Nadaju had to interrupt the show and make his pointless commentary.

Nadaju created his philosophical banter from misguided fortune cookies whose little pieces of paper he kept in an old humidor in his office. It isn't as crazy as it actually sounds. These little fortunes are written in a way to make them sound mystical and zen-like. They are usually positive and open for interpretation. Regardless how smart they might sound, they are just bullshit and for a man who makes his fortune selling bullshit to people, this bullshit is golden. Back to show.

"Yo, Adam. Wake the fuck up."

Adam, was quite startled. He shook his head, looked up at Chris and went back to staring at his computer to get back to work. At least to make it seem like he's working.

Chris continued down the hallway to finish his mail run. He stopped at Susan's cube.

"Sup Sue, what's going on?"

Susan raised her finger up in the air indicating for Chris to wait one second. She was talking to her mother. You could tell because most of the conversation sounded like this.

"Mom.....But, Mom....Mom. Listen. Ma. Listen for a second. Ma. Could you just. Ma, let me speak. I'll email you, goodbye." Then she hung up.

She finally put her finger down.

"So, what's going on there Chris?"

"You know the same ol' bullshit. This job sucks; I need to finish writing a damn paper for my stupid Western Civ class. My boss doesn't let me get any homework done back in the mailroom; even though, we have nothing else to do. I did everything that needed to be done, yet he finds something else for me to do. I swear I'm going to beat his ass, that lazy fuck. The work he gives me to do is shit that he should have had done himself last week. Asshole."

"Yeah he's definitely a lazy fuck. Every time I call him for something, he makes me wait for one of you guys to come back from your mail runs to take care of the problems. So what else is new?"

"Nothing, I'm too fucking busy for anything new to happen to me. I get up, go to work, go do homework, go to class, eat, shower, do some homework and go to sleep. It's the same routine Monday through Friday."

"What about your girlfriend?"

"She's a bitch. She knows I'm stressing out with everything and she still treats me like shit. Then she wonders why I end up cheating on her. You know? I hate being pissed off all the time. There shouldn't be a reason for me to be. This job is a piece of cake, school is easy, and I have a cute girlfriend."

"So what's the problem?"

"My boss is a gross, lazy bastard that doesn't care about my schooling. I have no time to work on any of my projects and my girlfriend doesn't support me by giving me head."

Suddenly, a voice came from the other side of the cubicle. "I'm going to get laid tonight." Chris was then pelted with a rolled up paper ball.

"Fuck you Adam. Who the hell are you fucking?" Chris looked over the wall and pegged Adam back with the ball.

"You know the blonde chick from personnel?"

Chris stared over Adam's shoulder, "You mean the one standing right behind you?"

Adam turned his head around nearly detaching it from his shoulders.

Chris and Susan started laughing. "Hey Adam," Chris said, "You better go to the hospital."

"Why is that Chris?" Adam, pissed off at the little prank, asked.

"Because, I just broke your neck."

"You're such an asshole. Go back to the mail-room."

"Blow me. Go back to staring at the little red light on your phone, psycho. At least I don't have to sit in a cubicle." Chris turned to look at Susan. "No offense Sue."

She just shrugged. No one likes sitting in a cubicle. That's why you don't find any at people's homes, because they are in charge at home. The boss never has to sit in a cubicle. If your boss does, that means he or she is one of the lesser of the bosses in command. Eventually, after looking up the corporate food chain and bypassing the shared offices, you shall reach the true boss, the one with the corner office with a window, a secretary, his own mailbox, the leather chair and mahogany desk at which he's never at.

"So Adam, you're going to bang the blonde from personnel?"

"Why yes I am." Adam was sporting a big "Cool Aid" smile on his face.

"She's no good for you man. She's too high maintenance."

"Chris, you're telling me that I can't handle a girl like that?"

"No, what I'm saying is that you **won't** be able to handle a girl like that. She needs certain attention. You need to feed on her every word and never seem distracted. I caught you staring at that damn telephone light before like a dumbass. You need to be able to seem like you care about what she has to say. Adam, I know you and there is no way that you care about what other people have to tell you. You don't get fazed."

Adam looked straight into Chris's eyes with an extreme look of concentration and interest and then proceeded to ask, "What?"

"Asshole, I know you heard me and were listening to me but you can't resist pulling off shit like that. She's going to be like 'Hey Adam, how's my dress?' and you're going to be like 'Well I must say that that dress looks stunning on you and it really accentuates your tits.' I'm telling you man, she won't put up with that shit."

"Maybe that's why your girlfriend doesn't want to blow you Chris." Susan was like usual, sharp.

"I'm not worried about that, there's always the girl from personnel."

"Fuck you." Adam pelted Chris with another paper ball.

"Blow me." Chris threw it back

"Let's go out drinking tonight." Susan mentioned the idea, still being on the ball like always.

"I'm down. How about you Adam? You want to come?"

"Well, I told that bitch that I'd call her."

"Well, then call the bitch when we're at the bar, that way we can scope her out. You know. Study her moves, her manners and see how much of a tight ass she really is. Come on it'll be fun. Come on." Chris put his hands together, like that hippy in all the church windows.

"Yeah Adam, come on." Susan gave him a look that was meant to motivate him with the idea that even if the blonde from personnel was a tool and stuck up, he might still get some ass.

"Alright, alright, I'll go. But, you guys better not be assholes." Adam agreed.

"Fuck you buddy. I'm offended by that comment especially coming from you. You know for a fact that we **will** be assholes. Plus you're the biggest asshole in the bunch. You're the 'King Asshole'. You should blow your nose with toilet paper."

"I do." Adam just shrugged his shoulders.

"You're an asshole." Chris replied.

Adam knew. How could he not have known? If he didn't know, then he would have been offended. He's not like the people that he hates; they hate what they are because they are afraid to see themselves in such a way that would contradict their lies. These people cannot stand to tolerate any inclinations that they may have the urge to be individuals. For Example take Chris from the Mailroom:

Chris was a twenty-two year old college student, who likes to party, watch CNN, sometimes starts a fight or two if someone hits on his girl, donates to the street musicians but not the winos, protests for human rights and equality, pays his taxes, votes, listens to punk music and jazz fusion and helps old ladies cross the street. "I just like to fuck and fuck shit up." Chris has been known to say on occasion.

Mr. Nadaju is a fifty-two year old lazy bastard, who never sees his children, makes millions of dollars a year, doesn't pay taxes, listens to no music, has one wife and three girlfriends, would piss on his own grandmother and has a comb-over.

The relevancy of this is that Chris was not allowed to have a Mohawk because it is considered unprofessional for the working environment and it may distract others from producing; however, he wouldn't shave it and threatened the company to sue them for discrimination. So the philosophical discussion is broken down to the difference between the Mohawk and the Comb-Over.

The Mohawk consists of shaving most of the hair from the side of the head and the top leaving just the crest with hair, a la DeNiro in Taxi Driver. It is obviously named for some dead red guys who loved to party hard and kick ass. The Comb-Over is more of a natural, yet still optional, hairdo. It occurs when the top of the head loses its hair, yet the eyes, within this head that the hair used to reside on, refuse to acknowledge that there is no hair left there. Therefore, what is done is that the person leaves the hair on one side of their head to grow long and then they proceed to comb it over the bald area, hence the name Comb-Over, until it meets the hair on the other side. This can be done from any part of the head that still has hair, even if all that's left was hair from the ears and eyebrows. This hairstyle is widely accepted amongst the rich and social elite. However, the Mohawk is not. Why?

Pure jealousy and nothing more is why. Imagine being a man that feels insecure for not having the hair on the top of his head, even though he has all the money in the world and can live as comfortably as he wants, and in walks the guy from the mailroom. He doesn't own shit, has no money, but is happy and is flaunting this thick mane on just the tip-top of his head. It could give you a heart attack. The comb-over was just as distracting and disruptive to business, especially anywhere with wind circulating, ceiling fans or central air conditioning.

The CEO cannot be happy not having the hair on the top of his head because he would be singled out as a bald man. The Mohawk is just a statement of individuality and not a form of mockery towards the bald, but it might be perceived that way to some. Chris would rather have a Mohawk, but would not be miserable if he couldn't have one. However, Mr. Nadaju would always be miserable instead of accepting his baldness, because he would never be able to have a Mohawk. Chris knew of men with this kind of mentality and that's why he fought to keep his. Just to piss off some rich guy with a comb-over.

If Adam were ashamed of being an asshole, then he too would be miserable, along with those others that he tried to make more miserable. Plus, his friends would consider him to be a total asshole and not as someone who was truly good deep down at heart. Adam's mother always told him that appearances are important. Adam preferred to appear like an asshole. That way people wouldn't get the wrong impression about him.

The World's Favorite Asshole

When Nadaju was setting up this reality show, "Rat Race", he had in mind to follow around a select few co-workers of Hardmega more often with the cameras. He picked out several people. One was the blonde from personnel because she's hot. Another was Chris, for being the guy in the mailroom who threatened to sue the company if it made him shave his Mohawk. There were a couple of more, like Lavash the security guard, if anything for nothing more but comic relief. The last guy they chose was the man with the most complaints filed against him at Human Resources, the one and only, Adam Stockton.

Surprisingly enough, people love to watch people like Adam do what he does best. The belittling of others is a fine art; when done properly it is entertaining to many different people. Some love the no bullshit attitude; others just love to hate those that are blatantly honest.

The network had been getting flooded by calls, letters, and e-mails from viewers who wanted to see more of Adam. There were also triple the amount of feedback from those that hated him so much that they couldn't wait to see him get his ass kicked by someone. Either way, Mr. Nadaju had made it part of his mission to exploit this opportunity as much as possible. A couple of weeks ago when Adam was at work, a tech crew bum rushed Adam's apartment and installed hidden cameras and microphones everywhere that they possibly could. Now the world could watch Adam's every move.

It was about 5pm, and Adam had just gotten back to his apartment. He kicks his left shoe unto the couch and then kicks his right shoe right out the open window.

"Fuck!" At twenty floors up, Adam just hoped he didn't kill anybody or break a car window as it drove by, forcing that person to swerve out of control, jump the curve running over a bunch of girl scouts that were accompanying a group of elderly women on their way to the children's hospital to give the cancer toddlers freshly baked cookies and brownies. No matter what, Adam wasn't going to check it out. He didn't need that on his conscious; but, just in case, he also unplugged his television and turned up his radio. That way he couldn't watch the horrible outcome on the news or hear any sirens.

He was more careful taking off the rest of his clothes. He put on a pair of shorts and his Yankees t-shirt, made himself a sandwich, grabbed a beer, sat down on his couch, after he tossed his one shoe aside, and pulled out a little box from under the couch. He finished the sandwich and his beer, went to the kitchen to put the plate in the dishwasher and grabbed another beer. He sat back down on his couch, opened the little box, pulled out his little glass pipe that his ex-girlfriend had bought him when they went to California one summer, packed it up, and toked up. He finished his beer and fell asleep on his couch.

Adam woke up to his phone ringing. He looked over at his clock and it said 9 o'clock. He picked up the phone, "Yer?" he had to clear his throat, "Um, Yeah? What's up?"

"Sup Adam? It's Chris."

Adam went to pick up his bowl as he talked, "Hey man, what's going on?" He took a hit as he waited for Chris to answer.

"Nothing, you still down to go out tonight?" Chris could hear Adam coughing up a lung. "Yo, are you okay?"

"Yeah dude," Adam was struggling to form complete words without coughing, "I'm (pause) O (pause) K. *Cough*. Dude, hold-up-while-I-grab-a-beer." He had to say without breathing.

"Alright." Chris didn't care waiting; he found a good spot on himself to scratch.

Adam took a swig and cleared his throat, "OK man, I'm good now. So yeah dude, I'm down to go get some beers.

"I talked to Susan on the instant messenger before and she's still down to go. I just have to give her a call to tell her where to meet us."

"Cool dude. When do you want to meet up?"

"How about at ten thirty in front of that new bar, the PLO?"

"Alright man, that sounds like a plan. That gives me enough time to shit, shave and shower."

"Yeah, I gotta do all that too. Alright see you at ten thirty. Peace."

"Peace."

Adam tried to motivate himself by stretching and yawning really loud, but the more he stretched the deeper he got himself into the couch and the more comfortable he got.

"Ok Dude! Get up!" He kept yelling at himself as he rolled over onto his side facing the back rest of the couch. "Uhhhh....." He started closing his eyes, "No! Get up! Get the Fuck up!" Adam got up, but a little too fast. All the blood in his body was still below his neck and the world started spinning, so he sat back down. He waited a quick minute before he lunged at getting up again. This time, there was enough balance in his blood distribution and he headed towards the bathroom with nothing more than a sleeping leg.

After shaving and standing in the shower for about forty minutes, Adam finally got dressed and made his way out the door. He made his way through the subway system unscratched and arose from the underground about a block away from the PLO. He lit up a cigarette and was done with it just as he arrived to his destination. There was Chris and Susan standing outside already. It was ten thirty-five.

"Dude, it's about fucking time you got here." Chris hated waiting. He always felt the urge to have to be somewhere and if he wasn't there, he felt as if he was missing out on something; even though he didn't know exactly where he had to be or what he was missing out on.

"Hey Susan, how's it going?" Adam just ignored Chris.

"Dick." Chris mumbled at Adam's disrespect.

"Good Adam. Hey, I can't stay out for too long and neither should you guys. We have to be at work tomorrow morning." Susan was the brains of the operation.

"Sue, that's what cocaine and caffeine is for, to help you through your day. You think the president has time to sleep? No. He gets all the good stuff we confiscate from Colombia like cocaine covered coffee beans. He's a busy man with lots of things to do." Adam eagerly said.

"You're retarded, you know for a fact that our President doesn't do shit but play golf and snort cocaine all day with his frat buddies. He doesn't sleep because he's strung out, not because he's hard at work." Chris was an angry punk. He hates it all. You name it, he hates it. Except for maybe good music, food, alcohol and women, but he's only human.

"So are we going into this place, or are we just going to bullshit all night out here?" Man would never get anywhere without a women telling him what to do; he'd also be a lot more comfortable doing what ever it was that he was doing that was making him happy before woman interrupted him. Susan was there to enforce the rule of "Man Shall not be Happy".

"Yeah let's check it out, I need a beer." Chris headed the way.

Chris always felt comfortable going into places, even places he'd never been in. It was his "hate everything" complex. He would walk into a place already ready to ask people "Do you think you're better than me?" He was fed up with everyone and everything already, even before he walked in. Susan and Adam followed Chris inside the bar.

Trendy bars in Manhattan are expected to be expensive; for those with little money on a Monday night it means that it should be an early night. For others who have the cash flow to spend on a Monday night at a trendy bar probably have jobs flexible enough to allow them to recuperate the next morning or not show up at all.

This bar seemed to be full of the type of people whose workdays did not require for them to be in anywhere the next morning. They were the very shabby-chic, posh and trendy type. All were very artsy fartsy and straight out of some hipster video. The eye candy was everywhere. All forms of beautiful people for all of our three companions.

"Alright, let's drink. What are you guys getting?" Chris, always very eager to drink, was itching for the bar.

"I'll have a beer; just get me the cheapest beer." Adam started to hand Chris ten dollars.

"Dude, in this place the cheapest beer is probably seven dollars. A mixed drink or something stronger is probably three dollars more and it'll get you a lot more fucked up. If you want to drink just beer, I know this great place that has dollar drafts all night long."

"Um…." Adam thought.

"Susan, what do you want?" Chris didn't wait for Adam's response.

"Let me get an L.I.T.."

"You see Adam? She has more balls that you do. She didn't ask for a beer or a regular fruity pussy drink. She ordered something that goes down like a champ and at the end of the night makes you dance on the tables. So what do you want?"

"Just get me whatever you're getting."

"Alright dude, good choice."

"So Adam, are you going to call that chick from personnel?"

"Yeah, but I kind of want to have a couple of drinks first before I do."

"If you call her now it wouldn't be too late for her to come out. If you hesitate, she might be at home getting ready to go to bed soon or even if she was already ready for bed, hopefully she is still awake and ready to go out. Also, you don't want to be too drunk by the time she gets here, that's pretty unattractive. So call her now and by the time she gets here, you'll be relaxed." said Susan.

"Alright, I'll call her up." Adam went outside to talk on his cell-phone.

As Adam finished up his brief conversation with the blonde from personnel, Chris was just arriving with their drinks. He placed each drink in front of its appropriate consumer's spot and took a seat at the table. Adam came in and sat down shortly afterwards.

"So what'd she say Adam?" Susan asked.

"Well she…." Before Adam could finish, he was interrupted by Chris.

"She? What she? Where? Hold up. Who said she said what?"

"Shut the fuck up Chris, you rooster looking freak. Comb your hair…" He then took a swig of whatever Chris had brought him. "pfffffff…..Oh shit. What the fuck?"

"Serves you right for calling me a freak. That, my man, is a Jack on the Rocks. It'll put some hair on your balls if you don't keep spewing it out like a little woman. No offense Susan."

"I'd kick your ass Chris, so none taken. Anyways, what'd the blonde say Adam?"

"She said she'll meet us here like in half an hour."

"Oh cool, good for you. But, Adam do you even know her name?"

"Ah nope, but I have a plan. When she gets here, before I get a chance to introduce her to you guys, Susan you get up and introduce yourself. That way she'll tell you her name out loud and then I'll know it."

"OK, I just hope it works."

"Of course it will, I thought of it."

"Hey, you guys ready for another drink? Adam? Yes. Susan? No. Ok, I'll get you one anyway, that way none of us has to get up later."

The drinks were going down easily. Chris stopped drinking Jack on the Rocks after having had five in about forty minutes and was now drinking whiskey sours. Susan was still on her second drink with another three in front of her that Chris kept bringing her every time he went up to the bar. Adam was still on his fourth Jack on the Rocks but was having some water in between.

"Fuck man, how much fuckin' longer do we have to fuckin' stay at this fuckin' bar? This place is fuckin' expensive." Chris wasn't digging the crowd too much. He tried mingling for a while and sparking up some kind of conversation with the people there but he kept getting pissed off and telling them something like "You guys are fuckin idiots!" or "You don't fuckin' know what your fuckin' talkin' about!" and he'd walk off.

Adam was getting wasted, so he wasn't realizing the potential trouble that Chris could start. However, Susan did. "Hey Chris, how about you sit down and help me drink some of these L.I.T.'s?"

"OK, I don't like the other people in this fuckin' place anyways. Hey Adam, so when was this broad coming? Hasn't it been like an hour already?"

"Yeah dude, shut the fuck up. If she ain't here in another twenty, I'll give her a call and let her know that we're leaving this place. In the meantime, how 'bout some shots?"

A couple shots of Maker's Mark, some shots of SoCo and Lime, Lemon drops, Mudslides, Sex on the beach, some tequila, a couple of more beers and an hour and a half later.

"Dude, we……gotta…..go. We waited, we gotta go now. We out." Chris's English vocabulary was quickly diminishing to a form only used by mentally retarded ESL students from northern Mongolia.

"Yeah man, let's get the fuck out of here. Fuck that blonde broad. She's a fuckin cunt, but whatever dude, we got wasted and that's always good. Yo, where the fuck is Susan?"

Susan got sick and tired of waiting for the boys to get wasted so she went in seek of suitable male companionship. When the boys are drinking, they regress to a lesser form of the male kind, a mix of the prepubescent male mind, the teenage boy's sex drive and the adult male's body. So there she was, speaking to an intelligent handsome man with a successful aura hovering over him.

"Come on Sue, we're fucking leaving this place." Chris told Susan as he grabbed her right arm with his hand.

"Hey buddy, maybe she's not ready to go." Said the successful handsome guy who seemed to Chris to be the kind of person who he'd like to hit.

"Come on Chris, let's go. Sue if you want to stay, that's cool. Give me a call if you want to meet up later or I'll see you tomorrow." Adam saw the look in Chris's eyes. Chris wasn't jealous or anything of that sort, but he had a really big problem with people acting tougher than he was. Chris isn't a stupid guy. He knows when he can't take someone on or when the person is truly tougher or crazier than he. But alcohol, well I don't think I need to explain to you all.

"No wait. Dude, how's it going my name is Chris." Chris extended his right hand for a hand shake.

"OK guy, whatever." The guy barely touched Chris's fingertips with his paws.

"Sue, you don't have to leave, but this guy is a douche bag and he's obviously a fag, just look at his shoes." As Chris said this, he never looked at Sue but stared at the guy with a big smile on his face.

"OK guys, let's just go. Hey man, nice meeting you. I have to go." Sue grabbed both Adam's and Chris's arm and pulled them out of the bar. As soon as they stepped out unto the street, the guy popped out of the door.

"Hey buddy, what the fuck is your problem?" He shoved Chris as he said this.

Chris looked behind him for a second, turned around and punched the guy. He caught the dude right on the chin. His knees crumbled and the guy dropped to the floor. Apparently the guy was tired, because he went right to sleep. So now this guy was in front of the bar totally passed out. Chris bent down to check if the guy was still alive. Susan and Adam were still in shock. No one said anything, except for, "Holy Shit." Who said it? Who cares? Chris placed his fingers over the guy's jugular vein and felt a pulse. This eased Chris's thought that he might have killed the guy. He felt less bad as he went in the guy's jacket real quickly and stole his wallet. Nobody saw him do it.

"Ok guys, let's get the fuck out of here. He's alive. I fuckin' checked."

"Chris. What the fuck, bro?" Adam was in awe. He couldn't believe that Chris laid this guy out with one punch. "Dude. Dude? What the fuck?"

"I can't believe you just punched him Chris. What the hell were you thinking?" Susan's lower jaw was hanging below her collar bone.

"He fuckin lunged at me, I was protecting myself. Okay? So, let's go. We need to leave now. I'm sorry. He's fuckin' okay. He'll live. Let's go." Now Chris was getting nervous, especially because someone was bound to come out of the bar sooner or later. Most likely sooner than later and knowing that he had the man's wallet in his possession, he felt rather uneasy. He grabbed Adam and Susan by their arms, pulled them around the corner and began to pick up the pace. They walked down three blocks before anyone had talked again.

"Chris, that was fucking great. OW!" Susan had punched Adam in the arm almost as hard as Chris had hit the guy. Then she hit Chris in the belly. He dropped to his knees and began puking all over the sidewalk. Sue saw this as an opportunity to yell at Chris while he felt like dying; that way he was to feel even worse for having done what he did.

"You fucking asshole! What the hell were you thinking, you stupid drunk bastard? God! You're such a fucking moron. You could have killed that guy." She then kicked Chris on his side forcing him to keep balanced on his knees by holding himself up against a tree that was next to him. He then continued to puke more profusely until he thought he was going to crack some ribs. Adam, during all of this, was directing passerby traffic. Some drunken chick had stopped to ask if Chris was okay.

Adam replied by saying, "Keep moving you fucking ugly ass bitch, before you join him."

She left.

"Oh God Susan. If I didn't like you, I'd kill you. Fuck. I need some water now." Chris finally got up from off the ground.

"You couldn't kill me; I'd kick your ass." She handed Chris a tissue so he could wipe the crust off his face.

"Thanks, just please don't hit me again." Susan threw a fake punch at Chris and saw that he flinched. This made her realize that he was sorry and she knew that he knew that she could beat his ass if she really wanted to. "Alright, so can we go get some beers now?" Chris looked over to Susan to get her approval.

"Don't look at me Chris. Let Adam decide."

"Shit, after seeing you beat the piss out of him we can do whatever you want us to do Sue." There was a slight pause that Adam felt was too awkward. "But nothing gay. I don't play like that."

"Damn it Adam, you're no fun." Susan said this as they all kept on walking down the block. They didn't know where they were heading to and they didn't know which one of them was leading them there. Regardless, they continued at an impressive pace for the next ten blocks before anyone of them spoke out.

"Wait, hold up. Where the fuck are we going?" Adam finally broke the silence and stopped the speed walking session.

"Alright look, I know this little dive bar about a block that way. It's shitty and ugly, but it's full of cheap liquor and good people. Plus they have a decent juke box and pool table."

Adam and Susan both agreed to go to wherever it was that Chris was taking them to. Sure enough, about a block down was an old beat up brown wooden door with a small diamond shaped window in it set way too high to actually look through. It was next to a red brick wall with a glass brick window containing a neon sign that said nothing else but "Bar". In they went.

The Night Continued

The inside of the bar wasn't impressive in any sense of the word. It was a dive just as Chris said it would be. The bar top was right across from the door as you walked in; there were a couple of tables off to the left, a couch to the far right and a pool table in the middle. The interesting thing about this place was its diverse array of people. They ranged from the hip rat pack swinger type to the hardcore punk rock type. In between was just about everything else. The funny thing was that they weren't separated into different groups. It was as if some supreme being went through the streets of this city grabbing handfuls of interesting people, threw them in a bag, shook them up and placed them in this bar. You had the blacks with the whites, the rich with the poor, the beautiful with the ugly, the old with the young, all just drinking, playing pool and socializing the night away.

Adam could tell that Chris was in his element. When Chris had walked into the other bar, the PLO, Adam noticed instant hostility in his eyes. Not because Chris hated the people at the PLO, which actually he really did, but because Chris knew that the people there would not try to make him not hate them. Chris walked over to Adam and Sue with three beers in his hands.

"Hey, I'm really sorry about before. It's that sometimes I feel like a rat in cage and I just can't put up with other people's stupid bullshit. Guys, I'm sorry. The rest of the night is on me." Well it wasn't really on Chris, it was on the guy that was taking a nap outside the PLO, but that wasn't important right now.

"Shit Chris, thanks a lot but you really don't make that much and I don't mind paying for my own drinks. Plus, I'm not mad at you anymore. I already beat the shit out of you; I don't need to rob you for your money too." Said Susan.

"Yeah Chris, you don't need to pay for us. Sue can pay for us. She's rich, just look at her shoes. Those are eighty-dollar shoes. She's a high roller."

"You're such an idiot Adam." Finally after all the drama, the group was back to their stupid immature ways. And, don't lose hope. Keep reading; it gets much worse.

"No. Look, don't worry about it. I played one of those dollar scratch-off things before we met up and I won like three hundred bucks. So it's all good. I got this. Besides, I know the fucking bartender and he hooks me up."

"Fuck it, I'm sold. How 'bout you Sue?"

"Shit, now I may be able to afford those ninety dollar shoes."

"Aight guys, let's go to a table and sit down, we've been trooping for days. Come on. There's an open table right over there."

As Adam and Sue turned to look at the table, Adam spotted someone familiar, someone that was obviously trying really hard not to be seen. "Speaking of shoes, there's that fucking bitch."

"Wait, what the fuck does she have to do with shoes?" Sue needed to know.

"I stepped on her shoe and that's how we started talking."

"Wow dude, you're fucking smooth with the ladies." Chris was determined to sit down, so he went off towards the table. Susan and Adam followed him. However, Adam didn't know whether to sit down or approach her. She obviously saw him, because she was trying really hard to seem like she didn't and their tables where way too close to each other. So the chance that they'd eventually be looking into each other's direction was very good. But, I'm just guessing. What the fuck do I know? Adam figured he'll go talk to her before he sat down.

"Yo, I'll sit down with you guys in a minute. I just have to do something real quick." Adam did his Saturday Night Fever walk towards the blonde from personnel's table, hidden behind a drunken stride. He posed right beside her, tapped her on the shoulder and with the most false grin and attitude said, "Hey, weird bumping into you here." He took a deep breath. "Yeah, because you were supposed to meet me at the PLO about two hours ago. So hey, what the fuck?"

I'm sure this was probably exactly why she was trying so hard not to be seen. Now she had to respond. "Well, I tried calling you."

"No you didn't."

"I did but I couldn't get through."

Not believable.

"You're full of shit." Not believing it.

"No really, I did try."

Still lying.

"So, why didn't you go to the PLO?" Still trying to get to the bottom of this.

"That's why I was trying to get in touch with you."

Liar.

"Now look and listen to me blonde chick from personnel. I don't give a rat's ass what you have to say to me. The bottom line is that you're fucked up. Shit happened because of your disregard for making your appointment. It's all your fault. So fuck off." Adam felt pretty good right about then.

Self-fulfillment can be so sweet unless you realize that you are truly a dumbass. However, until that point comes, you are on top. Your fifteen seconds of greatness.

"Adam, I'd like you to meet my parents. This is my mother Joan and this is my dad Jeff. They surprised me at my door after I talked to you on the phone. They flew in all the way from Seattle. I haven't seen them in five years. I totally forgot about our previous plans."

To all you men out there that are reading this right now; at some point in your lives you might have been hit in the "special area"; this pain is incredibly horrible. However, the pain of being extraordinarily humiliated while being extremely wasted is just as bad. They both make you nauseas and want to curl up into a little ball, while being exiled from the rest of the world.

"Um, I uh have. Um sorry. Hello sir. Hello mam. I apologize. I'm so sorry. I'm going to go now. I'm truly sorry. I'm, well, I'm, yeah, I'm going to go die now. I'll see you at work. Maybe. I'm sorry. Bye."

The question now was whether Adam should go to the bathroom and puke all over the place or go back to the bar and get some more drinks. So off Adam went to the bar. There was no need to waste all the booze that he has already consumed. Shit, people are dying on the streets of Bombay. Chris and Susan had been observing this whole little scene. Chris decided that this was the ideal time to cheer Adam up in his own particular way.

"Hey, Adam?"

"Yeah Chris?"

"Well Adam, I didn't know how to tell you before, but your puppy is dead."

"What the fuck are you talking about? I don't have a puppy."

"The reason that you don't have a puppy is because it was born dead and then later sold to a Chinese cuisine joint."

Adam stared at Chris for a while, trying to make an assessment of the things that came out of Chris's mouth. He lost hope trying, once his drink was placed in front of him by the bartender. Adam stared straight into his glass, twirling the ice with his fingers, and taking small sips through the little baby straw. He continued to zone out into the glass and finally spoke.

"What the fuck is wrong with you?" asked Adam.

"You're my problem Adam." Chris spoke with great seriousness. "My problem with you is this. Well Adam, the truth is I love you. I have always loved you and I want you to be with me. Adam will you be with me?"

Adam looked at Chris. He stared deep into his eyes and placed his hand on Chris's hand and gently began to squeeze it. He then asked Chris, once again, "What the fuck is wrong with you?"

"Adam, you don't love me?" Chris asked with puppy love eyes.

At that point Susan had walked over to the bar and broke up the emotional moment. "I knew you two fags were gay. That's why you two keep leaving me alone and not one of you have even tried to fucking hit on me. It's just my fucking luck that I go drinking with two guys and they're both fucking gay. Now let's order some more drinks. I guess I'm having a double shot of tequila and you two will be having white zinfandel spritzers."

Chris then stood up, grabbed Susan tightly by the shoulders, twirled her, leaned her back and laid a big kiss on her lips. He lifted her up, got on a knee and asked her to marry him. She looked at him and asked, "What the fuck is wrong with you?"

"That's what I fucking asked, 'What the fuck is wrong with you.' And he fucking proposed to me, kinda. At least he didn't kiss me."

"Well, I would have, but Sue killed the moment."

"Don't blame me. You guys can go ahead and kiss. I may find it hot."

Adam and Chris both felt that this little game was going too far beyond their heterosexual comfort zone. Luckily for them, they both turned towards the door when the most gorgeous woman in the world walked in to the bar. Every jaw dropped, every eye popped out their sockets and every tongue fell to the floor. You could hear in the background as she walked and took a step, "Bada Bing, Bada Boom, Bada Bing, Bada Boom." Hip to the left, hip to the right, every person at the bar was in awe. All gay men that saw turned straight, all straight women that watched turned gay. The smell of endorphins and lust was thick in the air.

"Dude, holy shit, dude. Dude." Chris kept elbowing Adam in the ribs and shaking Susan. Susan and Adam were so mesmerized that they didn't even notice Chris hitting them.

How and what exactly she looked like doesn't matter. She could have been black, white, Chinese, Indian, Polynesian. It doesn't matter. The only thing that matters is that she was impeccable. Her eyes, her feet, her legs, her stomach, her breast, her ass, the way she spoke, the way she smelled, the way she walked and held her glass were all perfect.

"That chick is mine." Adam told Chris with the utmost of confidence. This finally broke Chris's intense concentration that he was using to check out the hot chick.

"Dude, what about the chick from personnel? What happened with her? I thought I saw her in here."

"She dissed me to hang with her parents."

Chris then thought for a moment. "That's bullshit, man."

"Why the fuck is that? I saw them over there. Look, check them out over there at that table." He pointed them out.

"Okay, then answer me this one thing. If they are her parents, then why did she bring them to this bar? Not that there's anything wrong with going to a bar with your parents. But, this bar?"

"So what, Chris? Look, she's not from around here. She probably took them to the first place she found."

"Alright, that's fine. I just have one more question for you. Now I don't know where exactly they're from, but where in the non-rural United States is it acceptable for your mother to wear a see-through shirt with no bra, a leather mini-skirt, which even though I don't have the best eyesight in the world right now, I can see her panty-less crotch; while your father places his hand on your inner thigh, rubbing way to close to the glory hole? Now, you think about an answer to that while I go take a piss."

"Holy shit." Adam wasn't sure to be pissed off or turned on at what he was seeing. "Sue is that really what's happening over there?"

"Oh yeah Chris, your little girlfriend over there is about to get it on with her parents. Shit, I might too if my parents were that hot."

Adam looked up to Sue, "Sue that's disgusting."

"No Adam, that's not disgusting. The fact that you're getting a boner looking at your girlfriend with her parents is."

Sure enough, Adam looked down and saw that his little boy was beginning to grow up. "That's not because of them Sue, that's because you have such pretty eyes."

Sue looked at Adam like a chimp looking at one of those Magic Eyes paintings. "Put that thing away little guy. You might mess your pants."

Seconds later, Chris walked over with a huge smile and the hot chick by the hand. "Adam, Sue, I'd like you to meet Milay. She's a poli-sci student slash model. Also, if you might not have noticed already, she is extremely hot."

Susan and Adam couldn't respond, so they just stared and nodded their heads. Milay spoke out first, "So Chris tells me you guys work with him." Susan then held out her hand and said, "Hello". Then Adam tried to speak.

"Yeah, yeah we do. This is Susan and I am Adam. We work with Chris. You know, he works with us. We all work together."

"She knows that, dumbass. Chris just told her." Susan is always there to bring Adam back to reality.

"Yeah, hey guys we're just going to go talk for a little while over there, but I'll be right back soon enough." Chris still had the same smile on his face.

"Holy shit Sue, I can't believe that." Adam was in complete shock and denial at this point. "On that note, I'm heading home."

"Okay, I guess I'm going home alone, again." Susan said with an anxious subtlety in her voice, trying to hint Adam towards something in the after hours entertainment department. "Yeah, I should go home before I go home with the first guy who hits on me. You and Chris got me pretty drunk."

"Yeah, I'm pretty wasted. I'm going to say peace to Chris and the hot chick." Adam walked over to Chris, said his goodbyes to him and Milay. Then Adam walked out the door. Susan turned around to face the bar and finish her drink. A really greasy goomba sat down next to her and started to hit on her. That's when she decided that she really wasn't that drunk to just go home and sleep with any guy. She also didn't want to reach that point of drunkenness, so she made as if she accidentally spilled her drink on her suitor's lap, got up, apologized to him, walked over to Chris and Milay and said her goodbyes.

Chris stayed behind until closing, speaking to Milay. He got her phone number and a kiss on the cheek, then he walked her to a taxi and they went on their separate ways.

Work is for Chumps

Adam woke up, finally hearing his alarm after it had begun sounding off over an hour ago. He had no time to shave and shower if he was to make it to work on time. He smoked a bowl to rid him of his headache. He then had to brush his teeth and rinse twice to rid the taste of whiskey out of his mouth. He picked out some fresh smelling clothes from off his desk chair and got dressed. He put on his one shoe and started going crazy searching all over the apartment for his other, then he remembered it went out the window the day before; so he just put on his boots. Adam splashed on some cologne and off he went to race with the rest of the rats.

Adam thanked god for routine and the Pavlovian conditioning to which he had become accustomed. Today he had to totally go by instinct. He exited the elevator door of his apartment building onto the lobby as his race against tardiness began. First, Adam needed to fuel up. He went to the corner deli where he grabbed an "everything" bagel with cream cheese and a large black coffee.

An "everything" bagel is just what you would think it is; except, that it doesn't have everything in it. Instead it has a shit load of things on it. These things when eaten simultaneously, taste just like being one of the chosen people.

A shit load is a lot.

Adam also picked up the day's paper. Next checkpoint would be the subway. He had to fight his way through the crowd of slackers and of those who woke up in plenty of time to not have to rush to work. He knew that one of the subway's doors usually ends up just right off the third pillar. So, there he stood.

He heard the train coming and prepped himself for a tight full body insertion into the crowded belly of this tin beast. As it stopped, Adam realized that the train was stopping just short of its usual position. This time the door was just left of the third pillar. Adam made a mad dash around the pillar; he nearly spilled his coffee and lost half his newspaper. He just got into the tin can on time to get the last available seat on the train by pushing aside a slow elderly woman with a walker. The awful looks that he was receiving from the other commuters forced him to stand up and offer his seat to the old hag. All this moving around of his body and train wasn't making Adam feel too well, especially considering that he still felt the effects of the booze and most likely still was drunk.

After ten minutes of staring at "Piggy" and "Contribution", Adam was extremely glad to have had finally arrived at his stop. As soon as he left the terminal, he lit up a cigarette and finished his coffee; his bagel had long been gone. He walked cautiously across the block, making sure he followed every right step with a left.

He entered the first set of doors to his building of employment and much unnecessary distress, fumbled through his pockets to find his ID card to swipe in through the second set of doors, mumbled "hello" to the security guard Lavash and headed for the elevator. He got there with no problems and pressed the up button. He opened up what was left of his newspaper and began reading the headlines. This was a good way to avoid the "good-mornings" that everyone expects to receive everyday before eleven AM.

Being polite is very annoying. Being annoying is never polite.

On a morning like this, pretty much everyone and everything is really annoying. No wait, they're really fucking annoying. Adam headed straight for his cubicle dodging as many "good mornings" and "hellos" as he could. Those that he couldn't avoid eye contact with, where answered to with a swift nod of the head. A mere twitch of the neck and blink of the eyes was all that this greeting required a person to be able to do. It was pure automatic reaction; no thought or effort was needed. Adam figured that retards bob their heads like this all the time; it's why they're always happy, they never have to verbally greet people. These thoughts are the kinds of things that help one like Adam Stockton cope with such mornings.

Adam found his cube just where he had left it the day before, not that he was expecting it to be missing this particular morning, but he never knew. Everything was in place, even his uncomfortable, stinky chair, a godsend, his thrown, and his place of rest in this infernal place that he must call work.

"Good morning Adam. How are you feeling today?" Susan was peeking over from her side of their shared cube wall. She seemed fresh and invigorated.

"What the fuck is wrong with you? Jesus-fuckin'-H-Christ, bitch why are you so okay?" Adam kind of mumbled this in a just audible volume and raspy voice. All that mattered is that he could hear it and luckily Susan heard some of it too.

"Actually, I feel like shit too." Her whole persona shifted from full of life to seeming as if she had one foot in the grave. Then she smacked Adam upside the head. This of course made his brains spin inside his head as if it were laundry in an industrial size dryer. It took him a minute to regain his footing, and then he realized he was sitting down the whole time.

"What the fuck was that for?" Adam somehow felt obligated to know why.

"That's for fucking calling me a bitch, asshole." Though dead tired, Susan still carried a good smack.

"When the hell did I call you a bitch? Last night?" Adams brain was still settling.

"Just before, when I said good morning, you called me a bitch."

"Oh yeah, that's right." Adam really didn't remember, but why argue on a morning like this. Then Susan smacked him upside the head again.

"What the fuck? I'm pretty sure I didn't call you a bitch again." Now Adam's head was really pounding. He was getting kind of nauseous, too.

"Yeah, but you didn't apologize either."

"Okay. Geez, I'm sorry, just don't hit me again."

"Don't worry about it. I don't have anymore in me. I want to go back to sleep, but instead I have to go to some stupid ass meeting."

"Wow, sounds like fun. Just try to stay alive."

"Fuck you." She said this with her back towards Adam as she walked away.

Chris had been walking towards Adam from the opposite direction. He looked wasted still, however he did look a little bit more fresh than usual. It was very paradoxical, as if Chris actually looked more vibrant drunk than sober. This reminded Adam of the old kung-fu flicks about Drunken Wu-Tang, where the kung-fu master became stronger and could fight better when he was drunk. Adam has seen Chris drunk at work before after a night of drinking, but today he seemed way too happy to Adam. Chris pointed his right index finger at Adam and gave him a wink, and then he began to speak.

"Yo dude, guess what?" Chris asked Adam.

Adam flinched at first at the projection of sheer happiness that Chris had thrown at him. "What?" He thought about how Chris was going to rub it in his face about him hooking up with the extremely hot chick from the bar and was already regretting asking

"What?"

"I've got a job interview tomorrow."

"That's cool, what are you going to do?"

"Well, I guess I need to shave off my mohawk." In a drunken conversation, sometimes both parties don't quite understand what the other was asking or saying, however the conversation usually goes on pretty smoothly.

"Isn't that selling out?"

"Let me tell you something about my mohawk, Adam. It's a haircut. I like how it looks on me and I like that it makes people feel uncomfortable. Ninety percent of those kids you see on the streets and malls can afford to have a mohawk. Many of them are supported by their parents. I like not being dependant on my parents, but I also like not being on the streets. In this country, it's not whether you have a mohawk or three arms or an eye on your forehead which makes you not be accepted by society; it's how much you have in your checking account. I'll still go to shows. I'll still keep my political views. My life after work will not change. Hell, you pretty much do the same shit that I do after work. You and I didn't sell out. We were sucked in."

"Ain't that the truth? I never saw myself doing this for a living. I never wanted to go to college. Somehow I was coerced into believing that without a diploma, you couldn't amount to anything in this country. Do you want to know what I learned in college?"

"What?"

"I learned everything there is to know about sex and drugs and how to get free online porn and play beer pong. Do you want to know what the most important thing that I learned was?"

"Yeah, tell me. I'm dying to know."

"I learned that ninety-eight percent of people that graduate college are morons. They are clueless unoriginal, programmed monkeys. They couldn't point out their state's capital on a map, tell the difference between an Arab and an Indian, or tell you who the secretary of state is. All they care about is making a buck and believing everything their higher ups tell them."

"You think we'll ever be like them?"

"If we're lucky Chris, we will. You see, people like us suffer for the stupidity in this world. We are ashamed, embarrassed and angry at all this puritanical and moral bullshit that we consider part of the American dream."

"Yeah and as a result of all that bullshit, we drink, fight, act like assholes and sleep around. Not because it makes us feel any better but because we have this obligation to eat the meek."

"No one is holier then us."

Chris and Adam look at each other as they boasted about their superiority over the world. Then they both burst out in laughter. Adam spoke first, "We're so full of shit."

"Yeah Adam, but it is holy shit." You could almost hear the drummer hit the snare after that joke. It was so bad that neither Chris nor Adam laughed. Chris was actually a little embarrassed after saying it. "Well, anyways, before I forget, here you go. You finally got some mail that isn't interoffice."

Chris tossed Adam a small envelope with Adam's name and work address on it printed by a machine in script, just like a senator's signature after he replies to the letter you wrote him when you were drunk one night. On the back of the letter was a P.O. Box address from somewhere in Vermont.

"It must be important," said Chris "it says 'Mr. Adam Stockton.'"

Adam inspected the letter cautiously, flipping it over several times on his desk and reading the addresses over and over each time. "I hope there's no anthrax in this." Chris just looked at Adam and didn't say a word. Adam recognized that face from when his father used to make it to him, back when Adam would lie about finding his father's porno collection. "Okay fine, I'll open it already. It's probably a coupon for dry cleaning or a carwash. Hopefully it's for a Swedish massage."

"You mean oriental."

"No, I think it's Swedish; but that's besides the point, it won't be either." Adam said this as he used the blade on his Swiss army knife to slice open the envelope. Inside was a card perforated vertically down the center. The card was actually two passes to a screening for a new experimental theatre called "Random Observations."

Adam didn't seem too enthusiastic, so Chris snatched the card from him and began to read it. "Yo, it's this Friday. Are you going to go?"

Adam was still trying to think about what he had just read. His thought process still needed time to recuperate. "I don't know. I have no one to go with and…"

"I'll go with you." Chris seemed enthusiastic about it.

"Dude, shouldn't you be going out with that extremely hot broad on Friday? I'll give you guys the tickets and you two could go."

"No, you're coming with me. I'll meet up with her later. I'll tell her to bring a friend for you."

"Okay, but you better make sure that her friend is as hot as she is."

"Why is that Adam? Because the girl that you're banging is so freaking hot? Oh wait, you haven't gotten laid in a year even with pussy staring you right in the face."

"First of all, it's been only six months and I've been busy and what pussy are you talking about?"

"Dumbass, you've been busy playing with yourself. I'm going to tell Milay to bring a good looking friend that will put out after a couple of drinks."

"So you're saying that a girl needs to have a couple of drinks to have sex with me?"

"You know what, dude? Give me the fucking tickets. I'll take Milay and you can go fuck yourself for the four hundredth Friday in a row. What do you think about that, dookie?"

"You're gay. We'll go Friday. Milay met me; I trust that she can bring an adequate female for me. Anyways, it's only Tuesday, we'll talk about the plans before then."

"Alright man, though I can't call Milay yet. I kind of still have a girlfriend that I need to ditch and I don't want to seem too anxious."

"No you don't seem anxious at all; just extremely eager to dump your girlfriend already."

"Dude, just because you go out with a girl it doesn't mean the she's the one for you. Milay is smart, funny, and, not to mention, extremely hot. You don't turn down a filet mignon, just because you have a candy bar in your pocket. You eat it right up and enjoy it."

"Yo, I'm hungry." Adam stood up.

"Yeah, me too. Let's go get some food."

Their journey had begun, "a quest for food". There bodies ached as they walked past the legendary walls of the Cubicles. It was a dangerous excursion for the both of them. Chris, the tosser of mail, needed to finish the rest of his mail-run before he could enter the Cafeteria. Adam, an asshole amongst men, needed to avoid being seen by one of his many bosses, because indeed Adam was leaving his post ten minutes too early. Both men moved with much swiftness and agility. Adam and Chris would crisscross each other as Chris had to deliver mail on both sides. Chris would hand Adam some mail. Adam would toss it. He didn't care where it landed for it wasn't his job and

Chris didn't care because he didn't do it. Five minutes later they had arrived.

The Cafeteria was full of famished creatures. Many of which, considering their size, would definitely deplete the Cafeteria of its food source. It was a breeding ground for heart disease and obesity. Stress and boredom in an office setting can produce hunger in many people. That hunger turns to over eating. That over eating, in addition to sitting on your ass all day at your cubicle, produces weight gain. Weight gain, stress and boredom produce lethargy. A lack of exercise and healthy eating habits along with stress has created these short-lived gentle creatures that Adam and Chris found scavenging the aisles of the Cafeteria.

"Take a good look Chris. Take a good look at what your future has in store for you if you get an office job. I've already accepted my dismal ending. You should too."

"Fuck you." Chris knew this was true, what Adam had said. He knew that once he was in the company he would get comfortable, conform and accept all that he swore to himself he would rebel against. Millions of hippies did it before him and now he would be on the next wave of non-conformists to sell out or as the yuppies like to say "buy in".

Chris and Adam finally settled on buying the fried chicken and macaroni and cheese. They found a table close enough to the cafeteria entrance, so that they could watch the people come in, but not too close that everyone walking in could watch them eat. Neither of the two spoke as they ate. They didn't even complain about the dry chicken and the flavorless macaroni and cheese. They stared at all the good looking and healthy people walking in seemingly being followed by themselves, as they will appear in the not-so-distant future. They both ate quickly and sat there for a while, just sulking about their unfortunate future.

"Adam, what should I do?"

Adam was almost startled; he was so eagerly focused on the people walking in. "What do you mean?"

"Should I take the job or not?"

"First of all, I don't want to be held accountable for your life's decisions and secondly, misery loves company. So I would love for you to be in the same shit predicament in which I find myself."

"When you were a little kid, did you ever look into the future and see yourself as something or someone?"

"Sure, I saw myself being Indiana Jones. I wanted to be an archeologist and fight Nazis and voodoo doctors. Then, I figured in High School that there was no money in that. Now I'm making the huge bucks, my dumb ass. How about yourself?"

"I saw myself being president of the world, not only of the United States, but the whole world."

"Well, if you ever become president of the world, do me a favor and make me an honorary archeologist and send me to fight Nazis."

Chris nodded in agreement. They both grabbed their empty trays and placed them on the overly filled trashcans. They then went outside to smoke a cigarette and headed back inside to their respective desks for the rest of the workday.

What's Real?

As you all might have guessed by now, the show "Rat Race" is **now** entirely about Adam Stockton. There are plenty of fans of other people on the show that write in and request more of their favorite personalities, but since the viewer demand for Adam has avalanched over them all, they are left only for brief cameos. Of course it would only be if, and only if, Adam actually ever interacted with them. Regardless, the producers always have the final say in what is actually aired, mainly, Pierre Nadaju. Adam has all the potential for future exploitation that could make Mr. Nadaju a lot of money. Adam would get a substantial sum as well, but he's only doing all the work.

So now we watch the next day as Adam wakes up sweating and panting for air. He turns over just in time to see his alarm clock turn to six AM. He shuts it off immediately and gets right out of bed. He does everything he has to do this morning. He shits, shaves, showers, irons his clothes, gets dressed and even makes himself some breakfast. Now, he heads out the door, buys the paper, gets on his train and goes off to work. He isn't even trying to avoid people's "good mornings" today, he just ignores them.

Adam had wanted today to be over ever since he went to bed the night before and now that he had awoken from his dreaming and actually ventured into the day's journey, he wished he had never had gone to sleep. Maybe he wished he had never woken up, Adam really couldn't figure it out. He didn't like to mention it much but he was more able to deal with the world when he was wasted or recovering from a drinking binge. He was ashamed of this because it made him feel like an alcoholic. However it wasn't booze that he quenched for; he didn't feel the need to have to drink. Adam did feel that he needed to be doing something else at all times. There were few times when he didn't feel this way; when he was outside, wherever it might be, enjoying the breeze, talking to a girl, living his live the way he felt it adequate. Those times were rare.

Mr. Pierre Nadaju was watching Adam on the monitors in the control room. He gaily anticipated Adam's next move. He had been watching Adam personally almost around the clock. He learned to distinguish between Adam's many moods and the ways that he displayed them. He knew that Adam was dreading his every existence within the walls of that cubicle.

Nadaju thought out loud, *"Well, too bad Adam. You are part of a society with rules and regulations. You can't do what you want all the time. There is a mechanism that controls every aspect of your life since the moment you were born. You are a cog; you were put here on earth for a reason. You are not special. No one is special Nobody is an individual, no matter how unique they are. Compared to the large scale of things, Adam Stockton is nothing. Adam Stockton is not in control. Chris is not in control. Susan is not in control. Here, there is only one person in control and that is me.*

Now Adam, find out Chris's and Susan's last names for me, god damn it. You think you are the only one worthy of a last name on this show?"

Adam began to bug out. He wasn't hearing things, but he might have heard something. He didn't know. He's been feeling weird all day and the day had only started. He walked towards his desk. On his way, he checked Susan's last name on her nameplate outside her cubicle. "Susana Sorace" Adam noticed that it was the same name that he has seen written on that plate for the past two years.

"Good morning Adam, how are you?" Susan had snuck up on Adam as he stared at her nameplate as if were an aquarium filled with colorful tropical fish.

"Shit, Sue, I'm really out of it today." Adam wondered whether he had just called Susan a certain breed of gay dog.

"Oh so you were out drinking last night and you didn't even invite me to come. I understand I'm not cool enough to hang with you."

"No Sue, I didn't even go out last night. I don't know I had a weird dream. I don't know how to explain it. Maybe if I remember more later, I'll tell you about it. I'm going to go veg out at my desk for a while." Adam walked over with his head drooping low and sat at his desk. He turned on his computer and just stared at his monitor. Susan popped up from the other side of the wall.

"You know; all you need is to relax a little bit. The past couple of days you've been acting weird. You're usually funny and sarcastic, but lately you're kind of boring. You better get yourself together before it starts affecting your job."

Adam felt as if he had just stepped on dog shit while walking on the moon. What did one thing have to do with the other? He wasn't going to try to figure it out, at least not this second. "Okay, I'll make sure I stay witty." Susan nodded and sat back down at her desk. Adam just shrugged her off and continued staring off into space. Adam wouldn't mind being in outer space right now. He could just keep his mind blank as he took in the experience of floating between nothingness and eternity; just drifting away further and further towards a new galaxy. Unfortunately, he sat at his desk in his cubicle at the office in Manhattan on earth. Adam wished he could have just stepped on shit on the moon.

"What the hell is Chris's last name? What the hell is he doing? Do something Adam. Be entertaining, the whole world is waiting."

That would be Nadaju being Nadaju, cheering on Adam Stockton, watching the dollar signs flash across the screens. Right now, his only distraction was the oscillating fan behind him. Every twenty seconds it would make his comb-over turn upright. This is the kind of shit that really should be caught on camera.

Adam checked his shoe to see if he had stepped on some shit. He then went into his top drawer and ate two aspirins and two antacids. Strangely enough he actually began to do some work. He saw the little red message light on his telephone blinking, but Adam felt too uneager to check his messages. As they say, "no news is good news".

An hour later, Adam felt a smack on the back of his head. It was Chris.

"Yo Chris, what's your last name?" Adam spurted this out without even realizing yet that it was Chris that had hit him.

"*Good Adam.*" Nadaju said.

"It's Gomez. My name is Chris Gomez. Why'd you ask? Am I being invited to your Christmas party?"

"Yeah I'm going to start planning it four months in advance. I'm having a huge Christmas party. Then after all you guys leave, I'm inviting all my black friends for a Kwanzaa party. I just asked for your last name because you never told me before. Gomez, I thought you were Italian."

"No dude, I'm Puerto Rican. I don't look anything Italian."

"I don't know. Italian, Puerto Rican, same shit to me. I don't even know where the fuck I am half the time, especially today. I'm all out of it."

"You know what dude? Me too. I had some fucked up dreams last night. I can't even explain them."

"Yeah, same here. I had some weird dream about the theater thing we're supposed to go to on Friday. I don't think we should go. I have a bad feeling."

"Nah dude, I'm pretty sure they're unrelated. Your brain dreams of shit that you desire or that has been on your mind that day before going to bed. You were tired all day yesterday from the night before and you got those passes. We talked about it. It's just a subconscious manipulation of your thoughts."

"It may be. I don't know. All I know is that this dream was weird, man. You and I go to the theater and we sit down, you're to my left. There was an Orchestra playing, but it's really small, there were only about eight, maybe nine people in it. The theater was also small, maybe seventy people fit in it, but all I could remember were about twenty people being there. To my right was some chick in like a nightgown or something with her mom and her two sisters. They were all wearing nightgowns."

"What the fuck was I wearing?" Chris hoped that he would be wearing something halfway decent to the theater.

"I don't know. Black shirt and pants, same shit you always wear. Let me finish telling you my dream now."

"Okay."

"So, the lights go off and the movie goes on, but I'm not paying too much attention to the movie. The girl to my right was rubbing my leg and inner thigh…."

"Yeah, we can't go to the theater on Friday in case that happens. You fag."

"Shut up dick, I wasn't finished. So she's rubbing my leg and I'm like, 'Cool' but it's kind of weird because her mom was right there next to her. The little that I do remember of the movie, kind of reminded me of that Monkee's movie "Head" or that movie by Dali "Un Chien Andaleu". I mean it was totally tripped out. Then the people sitting next to you start talking really loud and being obnoxious. They looked like a biker white trash couple. You keep shushing them, but they won't shut up. So finally you snap and start yelling at them."

"Fuck yeah. Damn fucking bastards talking during the show." Chris shouted.

"Meanwhile, the girl next to me was nibbling on my ear and rubbing my leg and chest. I was only wearing my boxers at this point, which was what I was wearing in bed. Then the conductor of the orchestra says something to the usher, he stops playing, the movie stops and the usher heads over to us. There girl was tugging at me. The couple was yelling at you. The usher was screaming at us, saying 'You're not paying attention! You're not paying attention!' The conductor was booing us. We're trying to explain that it wasn't our fault and that we really were paying attention, but we get kicked out. Then we realize that it was part of the show. We were part of the show."

"So how would that make you think that it isn't safe to go to the theater on Friday? To me, that dream sounds like it was actually fun."

"Chris you don't understand, there was some other shit afterwards that I can't remember, but it left me not feeling right today."

"That reminds me of my Saturday nights and Sunday mornings. Dude, I was dreaming with some fucked up shit last night too. It was like I was watching TV and the TV started saying my name and there I was on TV, live. But I was like 'how can I be there live, if I'm here right now?' It was some fucked up shit, but I'm not going to stop watching TV now. So on Friday, we are still going to go to the theater. We'll smoke up and drink some beers before going. It'll be fun."

"Shit, you sold me. I guess we're still going."

A part of being an office setting employee is finding new ways to entertain one's self. Adam had become an expert at this. He had created more games using paperclips and staples than anyone else on earth. He even created little trinkets using nothing but office supplies. The trick to slacking off at work is to always seem as if you are working. He enjoyed his games, however, his favorite past time at work involved Adam typing messages about himself in third person on the word processor program on his computer. He would type:

Adam Stockton is a regular guy with a regular face and a regular body. He has a regular mind and an angry tongue. He knows what is right and you are wrong. So you are wrong to think you are right. If you say you are right, Adam Stockton you will fight. Work is bad. Adam doesn't like his job. His job is boring. He is going insane. He is losing his brain.

After a couple of hours of entertaining himself with mindless ranting and pointless games, Adam did some work just for a long enough time to make it seem to others that he actually worked all day. Adam's job mainly consisted of doing his boss's job by giving the work that he was given to do to the office temps. After all, why should he get stuck with the work when he's not even at the bottom of the corporate food chain? The hardest part about having a job in Adam's mind is that it interfered with his sleeping habit. Having to go to work is bad enough, but having to go before noon is strictly ridiculous in Adam's mind.

"Hey Adam, what's going on, my man?" It was John or Jacob or Jimmy. Adam looked up from his desk and nodded to demonstrate that he acknowledged his appearance. "So Adam, did you get my memo? I had left it on your desk." Adam didn't remember any memo being on his desk. So he dug around the mess on the top of his desk until he came upon a paper football that seemed to be created from a piece of paper that at one time or another in its timeline was actually a memo. He removed the piece of tape he had placed on it to keep it from opening up every time that he punted it with his middle finger through and in between the field goal he had made out of letter openers and plastic straws. He opened it up and read the memo.

From the desk of John Donald McCoist:

We will be holding a meeting on this Thursday, August 30th at 1:30pm in conference room 3Q. Please bring a note pad and writing instrument. This meeting is of the utmost importance so please do not miss it.

"Um, okay I'll be there at 2:30 this afternoon. I'll make sure I bring my pen and notepad as you asked in the note."

"Well you see Adam there's a little problem."

"What's that? You're changing the conference room in which it will be held?"

"No, the problem is that today is Friday, September 1st. You missed the meeting Adam and to top it off it's about a quarter to three in the afternoon. Where the hell is your head? Are you on drugs or something?"

"Okay, first of all, are you my boss?"

"No."

"Are you my supervisor?"

"Well no, I'm not, but…"

"Well then John McDonald, leave me the fuck alone. Can't you see I'm busy?"

"*Don't take shit from anyone.*" Nadaju's mouth began to water.

"My name is John Donald McCoist. It's written right there on the memo you're holding."

"This memo?" Adam looked down at it.

"Yes that memo." Adam could tell by John's tone of voice that he was getting angry. So Adam gave him the "hold on" gesture with his index finger. He turned around to face his desk, fumbled around with the memo for ten seconds and turned back around to face John. Adam placed the memo, which he folded back into the shape of a paper football, on his knee and flicked it with his right middle finger, hitting John directly on the forehead. John was speechless. Adam once again reminded him to "fuck off" and John did. Adam returned to writing his name in block letters on his desk calendar. He then remembered what John had told him about the date and time as he stared at his calendar. Today was the theater screening show. Adam had another hour to go until he was officially off of work for the weekend, so he got his stuff together and decided to leave an hour early.

Things are a lot easier and run a little smoother when you have a little bit of extra time. An hour during the workweek, during working hours, is a godsend. The streets are a little emptier, the stores are not as busy and the banks are still open. It is the perfect opportunity for Adam to take care of his business. Normally, he would do these things during his designated lunch period and when he has, he didn't have time to eat lunch.

A hungry mind is useless. A useless mind is, well it's useless. "I think therefore I am" "You are what you eat." So you think because you eat. Adam could care less whether he was able to process thoughts or not. He just knew that his belly was hungry. So he ate and now was.

It was a nice day outside, so Adam decided to walk home. He lived only a mile from where he worked. His stroll was going well until he realized that his shoes were not really suited for walking. Adam cursed the person that declared it inappropriate for casual wear to be worn in an office setting. Why would you want to be uncomfortable at work? Some jobs require attire that feel uncomfortable but serve a total purpose. They might protect you from hazardous material like monkey feces or homeless people. At Adam's job, a tie around your neck is sought after. A tie around your head or arm is not too popular in the eyes of upper management and neither are sneakers. Except on casual Friday, which it was, but Adam had thought it was Wednesday or Thursday.

The discomfort was too much for Adam to bear, so he went down to the closest subway station and caught the next ride home.

He arrived at home at about the same time that he normally would be leaving his job, three forty-five. He kicked off his shoes; this time making sure his window was closed first. Since it was Friday, Adam decided that this was a good time to take a shower and rest a little before going out that night.

Meanwhile, Chris was still at work. He realized, not to long after speaking with Adam, that it was Friday. Somehow, they are both equally as absent-minded and retarded.

Chris tried to kill some time before he was allowed to leave at four thirty. He would walk around the empty offices stealing pens and unplugging computers. Every now and then he would see someone that was staying late and would sit down to chat with them. There is a dilemma that many people run into on their daily routine. Sometimes there are many pockets of time in which the person may actually not have any work to do. This may make the person bored. However, should a person actually go out and seek more work that needs to be done? Should a person substitute boredom with work? Chris challenged his boredom by making up work that wasn't needed to be done. In actuality, he was only creating more work for someone else to do. Chris left.

Adam was just getting out of the shower. He dried himself off quickly, focusing extra attention on his genitalia. "There is nothing worse then crotch rot." Adam thought to himself. After he was done molesting himself with his towel, he went over to his couch and sat down. He pulled out his little box from underneath the table. He pulled out his stash and a Dutch Master vanilla cigar. He broke up about a gram of that sticky icky funky green shit and placed it aside. He then grabbed the cigar, moistened the outside of it with his tongue and lips and bit the butt end of it off. Adam then carefully undid the outside leaf from the cigar and placed it on the table. He licked the seam on the inside paper of the cigar and with his thumbs split it open. He dumped all the tobacco into a small trashcan he had next to him and ripped off a piece of the paper to make it smaller.

Then he dumped the herb into the paper and rolled it up like a joint. He grabbed the leaf and placed it on the table and moistened it with his spit. He then rolled the leaf around the cigar paper joint and removed any excess leaf from it.

Adam stared at it for a little while and marveled at his extraordinary accomplishment. He even said out loud to himself, "If I do say so myself, that is a nice blunt." He picked up his phone and dialed up Chris's cell phone number.

"Yo." Chris had picked up after the first ring.

"Sup dude? It's Adam."

"Oh hey man, I just got off work. I see you left a little early today."

"Yeah, I was fucking bored so I decided to leave early. That John McCoist dude was pissing me off."

"Why is that? He's a tool, but a nice guy."

"I'll tell you later. What you need to do now is get your ass over here so we can smoke this 'L'."

"Aight, I'll be there like in an hour, I need to go home first and shit, shave and shower. You know, all that shit that women expect you to do before going out with them in public."

"Alright man I'll see you in a little. Peace."

"Peace." Chris hung up his phone as he was still walking in to his apartment.

In the meanwhile, Adam was deciding whether to put on his boxers already or wait to the last possible minute to cover himself up. He decided to wait until he was fully done air-drying and watched some television in the meantime. One and one half episodes of SpongeBob Square Pants later came the sound of someone pressing the intercom from downstairs. Chris had arrived and Adam still had no pants on. He ran over to the intercom and yelled, "Come up!" as he pressed the door-open button. Adam then rushed into his bedroom to grab his drawers and a pair of pants. He was still putting them on when his doorbell rang. Adam hopped to the door as he had only gotten one leg into his pants. He finally had both legs in as he approached to open the door.

Chris stood there on the other side of the door waving a bottle of Jack Daniels in front of Adam's face. Adam acknowledged Mr. Daniels' presence by grinning back at Chris. He then gestured for Chris and Mr. Daniels to enter his "crib". No words were spoken, no conversation was made; but the level of understanding between the two was unimaginable. Chris went inside and sat on the couch, removing the plastic seal off the bottle of booze. Adam grabbed two small glasses from his kitchen, placed a couple of ice cubes in each, walked over to the couch and placed the glasses on top of the coffee table in front of Chris.

Adam then walked into his bedroom to grab and put on a shirt. As he entered the living room once again, Chris tossed Adam the blunt and lighter that were sitting on the table. The two glasses were also filled up with booze and ice, one to the brim, the other showed signs of being sipped on. The CD player was turned on playing Richard Pryor's "That Nigger's Crazy" and the blazing and boozing commenced. This was Friday and it needed to be kicked off correctly. Down the hatch and up in smoke, Chris and Adam shall continue to toke.

Reality Sucks

The truth behind reality television is that it couldn't be any faker. There are either fake people placed into real situations or vice versa, real people placed into fake situations. It's all bullshit and so is all the shit that's about to happen to Adam and Chris. You see, Chris is also a very appealing character on the show. It just happens to work out great for the program that they both decided to hang out together. One is an asshole and the other is a prick, a combination like that made Mr. Nadaju's testicles twitch. So let's take a look again at what these gentlemen were up to.

Laughter and smoke filled the room. Adam wouldn't open the windows for ventilation, because he didn't want to offend his neighbors with the smell of pot, although he was pretty confident that they all smoked too. Instead, he would place a towel underneath his door and light incense by it and another by his living room window. He knew that the smell of incense was a sure indication that the smoking of marijuana was taking place. However, he felt that the smell of it was much less threatening. Stoned cold paranoia is a godforsaken bitch. The only phrases that were spoken during this session were, "this dude cracks me up" as Richard Pryor told joke after joke or "more whiskey and/or ice?", as the two drank on.

"Yo," Adam asked, "What time are we supposed to be at the theater?"

"Um, check the tickets dude. What time is it now?"

"It's quarter to seven. Let me go find those tickets." Adam went into his bedroom to search for them. They would have been much easier to find if only Adam weren't such a disorganized mess. He checked in drawers, on his bureaus, under his bed, and under the pile of clothes on his floor; he realized that they weren't in his room, so he went out into the living room. He searched all over his desk, on the coffee table, between the couch cushions, and on his entertainment system. He was about to check in the kitchen, when Chris came out of the bathroom holding the tickets in his hand.

"Where the fuck were they?" asked Adam.

"On top of your toilet, under the porno mags. Dude, you need newer magazines, those are like from ninety-four."

"I don't need to buy porn magazines anymore. I have broadband internet access. I get all the porno I need at the click of a button. Anyways, what time is the show?"

"It says here that doors open at quarter after seven and the show begins at eight." Chris handed the tickets to Adam. "Here you go."

"You want to have another drink and smoke a bowl and then head out?"

"How about I roll a joint and we smoke it on our way there. It's a nice night outside, plus I don't want to get too wasted before getting there. I'll fall asleep or do something stupid. We still have to meet up with Milay and her friend after the show."

"Sounds like a plan to me. Shit's on the table, roll it up and let's be out."

Two minutes later, the joint was rolled and Adam and Chris were heading out the door. The theater was located only three blocks from where Adam lived. So they needed to take the scenic route so that they could smoke their joint. They walked through a park and did what they had to do and still it was only about ten after. They headed towards the theater and arrived there at about seven-thirty, there wasn't much of a line outside. Adam and Chris just figured that most people were inside. They handed their passes to a plastic looking usher with pearly white teeth and krylon painted blonde hair. They ventured down a hall of mirrors; there weren't many people in front or behind them. In fact, there were only about ten other people that they could see around them.

Another plastic usher, this time with black hair, stood at the entrance to the theater, checking people's stubs making sure they belonged there. Chris thought it was a little bit peculiar considering that there was only one theater and their tickets had already been checked at the entrance. Since there was no assigned seating, Adam and Chris both decided to sit in the center of the middle row.

"So Adam, does the theater look like it did in your dream?" Chris whispered.

"Except for the fact that you ARE sitting to my left like in my dream, everything else is different. Look at the people to your left. It's a little old Asian couple, not some crazy bikers like in my dream and nobody is sitting to my right."

"Well, it's only seven-thirty. I'm pretty sure not everyone is in here yet. At least I hope not; this place is empty. I bet this is going to suck. Everyone else in here is super old. What the fuck is this thing called again?"

"I believe it's called 'Random Observations'."

"Great. Sounds great. Real fucking great. Wake me up if something cool happens."

"Dude, wake the fuck up. You're the one that wanted to come see this show. I wanted to stay home and do nothing."

"Alright I'll stay awake. You can go to sleep. I'll be look out."

"Look out for what?"

"For anything cool. If I see something cool, I'll wake your ass up."

"Okay, sounds like a plan. Oh shit, it's starting already."

The lights were becoming dim and a tall black man with a shaved head and small, round, wire-framed, red tinted glasses in a tuxedo stood up in front of the stage facing the audience. The orchestra was illuminated in the pits by spotlights. They began to play mellow soothing music. Once the lights were totally dimmed, a spotlight was shined upon the man standing up and he began to speak.

"Ladies and gentlemen, welcome to tonight's screening of a wondrous and special event. You will be introduced to all forms of visual stimulation, audio titillation, and mental exploration......"

"Dude, we should have tripped for this." Chris whispered to Adam.

"Hell yeah." Adam responded. The MC continued speaking.

".....All invitations were sent to a select few open-minded and free-spirited individuals whom we believe can attain certain enlightenment from such a uniquely high level of entertainment. Tonight, you shall all experience an extraordinary show. Enjoy."

The spotlight was taken off the speaker and directed towards the closed curtains on stage. The curtains opened and there stood a slim Asian man in leotards and a yo-yo in each hand. He started tossing them and retrieving them normally and began to go faster and faster. Once, he was twirling the yo-yo with lightening speed, the spotlight was turned off and ultraviolet strobe lights came on. It was almost like a laser light show, but maybe not as cool. Adam and Chris were beginning to doze off. The music the orchestra was playing was very relaxing and tranquil. Neither Adam nor Chris could keep their eyes open much longer. About twenty minutes later they both woke up to screaming and yelling. They looked up on stage and saw a fight going on. Adam and Chris didn't know if this was part of the show or if it was real. Either way, they decided to just sit back and watch.

All of a sudden, one of the six men, on stage that were fighting, pulled out a knife and started to stab another man repeatedly in the neck. There was blood gushing everywhere; all over the front row, all over the stage, on the curtains and the orchestra. Chris and Adam were awestruck. They couldn't tell whether this was the coolest thing ever, or if they were ashamed for thinking that this was the coolest thing ever. Then in midst brawl the curtains closed and a screen dropped down.

A movie started to play. It was one of those weird time-lapsed movies in which they show a carcass being decomposed by bugs and bacteria. Once the dead coyote carcass was fully decomposed, another short film started to play depicting two small children skipping hand in hand down the beach shore with their backs to the camera. This went on for a while until the kids were at a far distance. Adam and Chris started to doze off again during this part, until there was a loud explosion sound and film of nuclear weapon testing was shown. There was footage of buildings being destroyed and mushroom clouds, but the most disturbing images were of nuclear and radioactive victims being treated. They must have been from Hiroshima, Nagasaki and Chernobyl. There were scenes of people swollen with radiation; there skin burnt to a crisp, vomiting profusely, scenes of babies being born with deformities and abnormalities.

Just as Chris and Adam began to feel sick from all the images, the screen went up and the curtains opened. The spotlights went back on and there on stage stood three of the most beautiful women they had ever seen, nude, perfectly groomed and smoothly shaven. Adam and Chris could not believe their eyes. Their primitive animal instincts started to kick in. They began to salivate and their hearts began to palpitate. The women turned to face each other. They then began to touch each other and kiss one another.

"Holy fucking shit dude." Adam whispered to Chris, whom was sweating in his seat with a mixed expression on his face of lust, embarrassment, curiosity and intrigue. Which ever one it might have truly been, Chris's temperature was rising rapidly.

"Dude," Chris said to Adam, "Dude, dude, dude, dude, look, holy shit dude. Wow. This is the best show I have ever seen in my entire life. Now aren't you glad that we came. I wish I would have brought Milay to this, she might have gotten turned on and mentioned a threesome."

Adam wasn't listening. He was paying too much attention to the show being put on stage. This was the kind of stuff that he would go on the internet to watch live via webcam straight from Amsterdam or the Ukraine. Adam had now been transported into his own little fantasy world in his mind, where these kinds of acts are extremely common and celebrated within the community. One of the girls had put on an extremely large strap-on and was just about to mount another girl when the curtains closed and the screen dropped back down.

"God damn it. Let's get the fuck out of here." Adam said this before he looked around the theatre and realized that it was completely packed with people. They must have all came in when they were both passed out.

"Forget it; we're stuck in here for the rest of the show." Chris had an extreme look of frustration on his face. You could tell that the girl on girl action had woken him up from his stupor, but now they had taken that away from him. He was too alert to go to sleep and too bored to pay attention. The next video footages that they were showing were of animal testing done by some government or Tobacco Company, sticking armadillos under extremely hot flames and feeding botox to puppies, the kind of shit that Adam and Chris were used to watching at 3:30am on the public access channel. The rest of the show was a three-ring circus of disturbing films and freak show acts. People juggling chainsaws and getting their hands and fingers cut off, others piercing their bodies with swords and lifting stones with their nipple rings. Sure it was a good show, very sick and twisted, but Adam and Chris had seen it all already. This is America for God's sake, the land of perversion and idiocy. This kind of crazy shit is seen on the morning wake up show as they warn parents that this sick shit it out there to corrupt their children.

They were finally let out at around quarter to ten. There is an extreme fatigue that hits a person who has been sitting down in the same chair for two hours after a good session of drinks and herb. Neither Adam nor Chris really wanted to have to meet up with Milay and her friend anymore, they were more eager to go back home and play some video games. However, they knew they couldn't back out now and if they were going to catch their second wind they would need to start boozing again. Chris called Milay up on his cell phone and asked her if she wanted to meet up somewhere, or if she wanted them to pick her and her friend up. She told him that they should meet up at a little dive bar by the waterfront that was roughly the mid point from where they were all located. She told them that she and her friend would meet them there at approximately eleven o'clock.

Adam and Chris figured they'd get there early to commence their night of drinking and stupidity. They could have walked, but that would have wasted precious drinking time getting there, so instead they hopped on the subway and took the five-minute ride. As they waited and rode on the train, they realized that they haven't spoken to each other ever since the naked ladies went off the stage. It might have been a result of their fatigue combined with their mind's slow absorption of the images that had just been fed to them. Adam turned to Chris and decided that it was time to break the silence.

"So I've really been fucking up at work as of lately."

"How's that, your job is easy."

"Well, that's the thing. I've been working there for a while now, just about when you started working there, and I'm still not sure what my job is. I don't know if I'm a programmer or an administrative assistant. Shit, for all I know, I could be a boss. So as of lately, all I do is zone out all day long. I used to just do that for an hour or two a day, but lately it has been an all day ordeal. That reminds me.

Earlier today John Jacob McDonald or whatever-his-name-is asked me if I got his memo. I said I didn't know. It happened that I've been using it to play paper football for the past week or two and never bothered to read it. The memo was for a meeting yesterday. One thing led to another and I told him to fuck off and pegged him in the face with the football."

"Nice, what did he do?"

"Nothing, what was he supposed to do? Now get this, I think I'm getting a raise or something. I got a letter at home from the company, congratulating me for my good job and all that bullshit. It mentioned something about me getting compensated for my hard work. They must have gotten the wrong guy….."

Chris interrupted him, "Yo, before I forget. They're getting rid of my supervisor. That means I may be able to take over for him. I'd be getting his pay and doing his job, which I was already doing. Shit is hot as hell. Now I won't have to shave my mohawk off, but I probably will anyway; I kind of need a change."

The train stopped at the station and Adam and Chris got off, this was their stop. A street performer stood by the platform playing his saxophone with his case wide open, ready to accept the pocket change of passing by listeners. Chris and Adam stood there for a minute listening to the man play some true blues as the other passerby's did just that, pass by, an occasional quarter or dollar was thrown into the case. However, they stood there and listened to the whole song and each left the man five dollars before walking away.

"He was good." Adam told Chris as they walked out of the sub-terminal.

"Yeah and to think that he has to play in a subway station to make money, while all these fake-ass musicians litter our record stores, radio stations and MTV. This is why America is so fucked up, because people can't make their own decisions. We can get a piece of dog shit, dip it in gold, put a diamond on it and market the hell out of it and the general population would buy it as the new fad sensation. Popular culture is obviously crap because it requires mass marketing to sell it. That's why it's popular, not because it is good, but because everyone is brainwashed into thinking it is. Why do rappers drink Cristal Champagne? Because, they think it's cool. I've been drinking booze for a long time. I can't tell the difference between a five-dollar bottle of champagne and a two-hundred-dollar bottle. Shit all tastes the same to me and I bet it tastes the same to them too. However, you place it in the hands and fridge of every rapper and rock star from here to kingdom come and the shit sells like hot-cakes."

"Wait what? You lost me after popular culture; I was reading that billboard over there for that new spiked-iced tea drink thing. It looks disgusting. Whiskey and cherry flavored soda can't be good. That's just a headache in a bottle."

"You see, that's what I'm telling you. You won't buy into that shit because you make your own decisions, but others will just eat that up."

"Dude, even good products get advertised."

"Yeah, but they aren't forced fed to us. They're not on every page you turn to in a magazine or on every channel. It's fucked up. Man, I'm telling you this shit fucking pisses me off. I can't believe......."

Adam decided that he had heard enough from Chris and interrupted him. "Dude, shut the fuck up. There's the bar. Let's get drunk."

"Okay."

They had arrived at Kansas. That is the name of the bar, "Bar Kansas". It was full of yuppies and gays sipping on fruity drinks with umbrellas in glasses with salted rims. Chris and Adam felt out of their element. The place was decorated with images of the Wizard of Oz, each wall like a different scene. Dorothy over here, Toto over there, the Wizard behind the bar, there were flying monkeys everywhere. It looked like somebody had a strawberry, banana and Guinness milk shake and puked all over the place. Adam and Chris decided that the best thing to do was to stare at their reflections on the mirror behind the bar. They each ordered a pint of beer and a shot of whiskey. They took the shot and started drinking the pint.

"What the fuck is up with this place? Why would Milay ask us to come here, out of all the bars in this city? This is so gay." Adam noticed that the bartender, a drag queen in a Dorothy outfit with ruby slippers and all, heard him say that. "I'm sorry man, I didn't mean it as an insult. I'm just surprised that the two girls we are waiting for asked us to meet up with them here. I've never been here before. Not because I have a problem with gays, but because I'm not gay. You know what I mean?"

"Don't worry sweetie, I know what you mean. There are a lot worse things that people who have come in have said to me. I just have one question for you guys. How well do you know the girls you are both waiting for?" The drag queen bartender left them at that and went to the other side of the bar to help some other customers.

"Chris, how well do you know Milay?" Adam was starting to seem a little worried. "I mean, we were pretty drunk when we met her, if you know what I mean."

"No dude, shut up. Don't even say that. I would know. I would definitely know, no matter how much I drank." Chris chugged down his beer and ordered a Jack on the rocks.

"Dude, slow down. You don't want to make the same mistake twice. You keep it up and you might become a regular here." Adam looked up and made the facial expression equivalent for "I'm sorry" to the bartender. The bar tender wasn't fazed. He even filled up Adam's beer before he asked him to.

"Yo, she's a girl. I'm positive. I've been with enough girls to know that she is a female. There is no way in hell that a man can be that hot. Goddamn it dude. You know that's going to be the first thing I mention once she comes in here. Gay dudes are always hitting on me, no wonder a girl that hot finds me attractive. She's a guy. Damn it."

"Chill out man. I'm pretty sure she's a girl. What I'm worried about is that maybe she thought I was gay and is bringing a gay dude as my date."

"Well, whatever it is, you're not leaving. That'd just be rude."

"Rude is hooking me up with a guy. I don't want to be some dude's date. I don't mind if the guy hangs out, but I'm not going to be his date. Okay, you know what? Let's change the subject. I'm pretty sure it'll be a chick. She just picked this bar because it's at the halfway point."

"Yeah probably, cheers." They clanked their drinks together and simultaneously stared down into their glasses and sighed. Not because there was a problem with their drinks, but because they were tired of staring at themselves in the mirror. As Adam and Chris were almost done with their drinks, in walked in Milay, looking as hot as ever, and her friend. Her friend was a gorgeous blonde with a smoking body and the most impressive azure eyes that Adam had ever seen. You could tell that they must have been impressive when Adam noticed them even as she took off her jacket to reveal how scantly dressed she was. Adam and Chris just looked at each other and nodded once. They knew these were women; they didn't even have to ask.

Dorothy, the cross dressing bartender, leaned over to the guys and reassured the two. "Those are definitely real women."

Chris and Adam both stood up to greet the females. Chris gave Milay a kiss on the cheek and Adam shook her hand. She then stepped aside to introduce her friend.

"This is my friend Stacey. Stacey this is Chris and Adam." Chris had his arm around Milay, so he just waved hello. Adam was frozen in time and with him his speech. He knew that he tended to make an ass out of himself in front of women he found attractive. This time he figured that he would think about what he would say before he said it. After much thought, Adam was able to say, "Hello" and he shook her hand.

Chris could see that his friend was drowning, so he decided to break the ice a little. "So Milay, what is the deal with this bar? I mean, did you know that it was a Wizard of Oz themed bar?"

"I actually have never been in here before. I just figured we come check it out."

"That's okay, we don't mind. Ain't that right Adam?" How easily a man can forgive a pretty face, especially one it is attached to such a hot body. Adam just nodded his head, as he was still afraid of the direction that his words might take him.

"Um, yeah…So do you guys want to sit at the bar or at a booth?" Adam felt a sense of pride in his first successful attempt at communicating verbally. Everyone had agreed to sit at a booth, this way they would actually be able to face each other and converse without having to deal with the mirrors by the bar. In actuality, Milay and Chris felt that if they all sat at the bar Adam would pretty much try to ignore Stacey. Adam knew this was true, so he felt it appropriate to sit at a booth. The man wouldn't mind getting his pecker wet by such a fine female specimen. He knew that he might never get a second chance at such a trophy.

They all sat down, Adam opposite of Stacey on the inside of the booth and Chris opposite of Milay on the outside, so Adam wouldn't be able to wander off. Chris started a tab and brought back drinks for everyone from the bar, he tipped the over sized Dorothy. They usually give you more booze in the drinks or at least a couple of free ones if you tip them well. By they, I mean bartenders, not cross-dressers. Although, maybe them too.

For the most part, their time at Kansas was spent lamely. They had lame conversations, lame jokes, and shared lame anecdotes. Their time there was turning out to be a disaster. Luckily, Dorothy the Bartender had been putting plenty of booze in their mixed drinks. A sober mind would have grown tired of such a boring predicament. Adam and Chris began to reach their level of drunken Zen. This is where the mind is transported away from the body and it becomes one with the universe. Basically, it's when you start losing control or black out.

"Let's get the fuck out of here." Adam told the table, while nudging Chris to stand up and stop staring at Stacey. "I'm going to go pay the tab and then we need to head somewhere else." Adam was pretty fucked up at this point, and so was everybody else. He walked over to the bar and called for Dorothy to come to him. "Dorothy, baby, you've been great, but we have to leave now. Just tell me what we owe you so I can pay, but I promise that one day we will click our heels three times and come back to Kansas." Adam paid the bill. He then handed a ten-dollar bill over to Dorothy and as Dorothy tried to reach for it, Adam grabbed a hold of her/his hand and gave it a kiss in a very heterosexual creepy way. Dorothy was left shocked as Adam walked back to his friends, whom were waiting for him outside at this point.

"So where to, chieftain?" Chris asked the crowd of three. They all stared at each other and shrugged their shoulders. "Well, I don't quite want to go to a bar, but I do want to keep drinking. Yo Adam, you've got a pretty decent place, let's go back there to have a drink and a smoke and we'll make plans from there."

"Dude, if I go home I'm going to fall asleep. I don't want to pass out just yet." Adam was having a hard enough time keeping his eyes opened while standing up. "I need to keep moving around, so I can catch my second wind."

"Well, Stacey and I will make sure that you guys don't fall asleep anytime soon." Milay looked over and winked at Stacey. Stacey then grabbed Adam from the arm. Adam was caught off guard; he looked over at Stacey and smiled. He then shook his head violently and jumped up in the air, like a boxer prepping up before a fight.

"Whoo!" Adam finished shaking off his sleepiness and looked at Chris, then Milay and then Stacey. He grabbed a better hold of her and in a very 1980's teen movie cliché way said, "Let's party."

"Haha, okay Robin, let's go," Chris swung his arm forward and pointed towards the subway with his index finger, "to the bat cave."

They all started heading down the subway station stairs when a young man running up the stairs bumped into Adam, almost knocking him down, and kept on running.

"Yo asshole! What the fuck?!" Adam patted his jacket down to try to compose himself. It was brisk that night. He then realized his wallet was missing. "Mother fucker!!! He took my wallet!" Adam and

Chris ran up the stairs. As soon as they stepped out of the station entrance Adam tripped and fell. He looked down and saw that he had stepped and slipped on his wallet. He grabbed it and opened it up to see what the damage was. "What the fuck?"

"What'd he take?" Chris reached his hand out to help Adam get back up. The girls were just exiting the station onto the street.

"Yo, I had like sixteen bucks left after I paid the tab at the bar. Check this out." He pulled a wad of hundred dollar bills out of his wallet. "Dude, there's like a couple of grand in my wallet. I've never even seen this much money before." Chris still had his arm extended, and although he could still see Adam on the ground, he had totally forgotten why.

"Get up. Get up now and let's go. We'll figure this out elsewhere, but let us go now." Chris finally grabbed a hold of Adam's hand and yanked him up. "Adam, we're going to your place. I'm pretty sure you aren't going to pass out now."

"Yeah, let's go. I…..I……..I……." Adam couldn't figure out what was going on in his head because he didn't even know where to start the thought process.

"Just hold on to my belt and I'll drag you along. Just keep your wallet in your front pants pocket." Chris started pulling Adam down into the subway station. He waved to the girls to follow. Adam was just staggering down the stairs with his hand firmly placed on his wallet in his pants. Chris used his Metro card to swipe everyone through the turnstile. They all sat down on the same side of the train, Chris to Adam's left, Milay to Chris's left and Stacey to Adam's right. Not one of them spoke; they just waited for their stop and got up with synchronicity, as if choreographed.

They all sped walked the few blocks that separated the sub-station with Adam's apartment. When they got to the front door entrance, Adam fumbled around with his keys. He was using his left hand to open the door, because as a right hander, he had more confidence in his right hand to protect his wallet. After about ten minutes, Chris got frustrated and took the keys from out of Adam's hand and opened the door himself. They ran up the stairs and Chris took it upon himself to open the door to Adam's apartment.

As soon as the door was opened, they all flung into the apartment. Chris locked the door behind them using all the deadbolts and chain locks that had been placed and collected on the door since it was installed in the early 1960's. He then ran to the windows and shut all the shades. Adam went running to his couch and sat down, placing his wallet on his coffee table. Milay grabbed some clean glasses from the dishwasher, the bottle of Jack Daniels from the drawer above the sink and some ice from the freezer. She then brought them over to the table.

"Thanks babe," Chris grabbed his drink immediately, "good guess on finding the bottle?"

"I've been here before." she replied promptly.

"No you haven't. This is the first time you've ever been here, unless you and Adam have something to tell me."

"She's never been here before. I wish I were lying to you," Adam finally took his eyes off his wallet and looked up at Milay, "How did you know where the booze was?"

Stacey answered, "All men keep their booze in the same places, it's as if it were programmed in your heads. I would have found all your stuff too Chris. Keep focused, what's the deal up with you guys?"

Chris sat down next to Adam as Adam removed the wad of cash from out of his wallet. He then began to count how many bills he had, out loud. "One, two, three,....,ten, eleven,.....,twenty-three, twenty-four, twenty-five, twenty-six, twenty-seven. There's twenty-seven hundred dollars here. Some dude stole my wallet and put money in it. I...I....I...." He couldn't explain it.

"Dude, maybe it's dirty money. You know, like drug money or someone robbed it or it's counterfeit. You may get in trouble for having that money."

"So what should I do? Get rid of it?" Adam was gripping the money like a retarded child would hold a canary, tight enough to pop its head off.

"No man, that's just dumb. We need to spend it all tonight. We can be like rap stars only not as rich."

"Word up dog. We be the shiznet tonizzle, fo shizzle ma nizzle, aight." Adam pounded Chris's fist and barked like a dog, "Arrf, Arrf!"

"Ladies, we're getting fucked up tonight." Chris couldn't take the grin off his face. "Adam, who would have thought that two degenerates like us would be going out with that much cash and two hot broads? This is why we need to always carry camcorders around with us, because no one would ever believe us."

"Chris, let me talk to you for a second in my room." Adam grabbed Chris and excused himself to the girls. They walked into Adam's room, they didn't close the door but they stood where the girls couldn't see them.

"What's up Adam?"

"I'm going to give you a thousand dollars. I'm going to keep a thousand dollars in my wallet, two hundred in my shoe, three hundred in my back pants pocket and two hundred in this little pocket in my pants. I'm telling you this just incase I forget or I pass out or something. I was half way in the bag before this whole money thing happened. I don't know how coherent I'll be in a couple of hours."

"Dude, maybe one of the girl's should be responsible. I'm just going to get as wasted and I'll just run your pockets to spend it on more booze and strippers."

"Yeah, but I don't know them well enough to trust them; plus strippers and booze is a good reason to run my pockets. So let's have fun tonight," Adam got closer to Chris to whisper even softer, "I want to bang Stacey."

Chris whispered back, "Me too, I was hoping you passed out and then I could have both of them."

"Give me the thousand that I gave you back and I'll let you."

"Fuck you, I'll just wait till you pass out." Chris turned around and began heading out to the living room when he turned his torso around and said, "Come on, the girls are getting anxious and so am I."

The Best Things in Life are Free

Nadaju had decided to give these guy's all the possible resources to completely self-exploit themselves. The whole wallet situation would be completely unbelievable even to the most retarded back wood Chinese hillbilly, but luckily with the power of commercial breaks; Mr. Nadaju is able to remove anything that could actually falsify the reality of all the bullshit. He happily sat in one of the rolling chairs in the editing room with his feet up on a bench, leaning his head up ever so slightly, and squinting his eyes at the monitor. His head was tilting at just the right angle for gravity to take a hold on some of his floating bushels of thin long hairs. They perfectly stood vertically from Nadaju's exposed scalp giving him a rather pretty bad ass looking "liberty spikes" Mohawk.

Chris would be proud.

Adam, Chris, Milay and Stacey walked down the street; Chris to Adam's right, Milay on Chris's right and Stacey on Adam's left. The two males were radiating with confidence; they felt like Roy Jones Jr. would if he were told he was about to fight Michael J. Fox for the Light Heavy Weight Championship belt. They combed their surroundings. They were looking for a place where they normally wouldn't have gone into. Soon enough they spotted a club with black tinted glass windows and a blue neon light on a piece of steel shaped like a cat. Velvet ropes were arranged at the front door to keep out all "undesirables". The name of the club was "Pussy".

"Oh yeah, we're definitely going in here." Chris said mischievously as he walked up to the bouncer. He took out his driver's license to show the man that he was actually old enough to go into the establishment. The bouncer just looked at him and shook his head "no". Chris was not so much as shocked as he was angry. He turned around and went to grab one of the posts holding the velvet rope, but Milay stopped him before he could. Adam walked up to the bouncer, spoke to him and shook his hand, after only a brief moment.

"Okay, follow me." Adam waved the others to follow him into the club. The place was wall-to-wall plush velvet adorned with super models and money; bottles of Cristal were being passed around like food stamps in the ghetto. White teeth, platinum jewelry and hair glitter was all that could really be seen in the darkness of this plum dark atmosphere. Adam found a vacant lounge area and sat down.

"Yo, what'd you tell the bouncer!?" Chris yelled over to Adam who was sitting at the other side of the couch, Milay and Stacey sat between the both of them.

"I told him that you're in a famous underground punk band and you have a big ego and then I slipped him a hundred bucks. Money talks man. Bullshit mother fucking walks." Adam was then distracted by a gorgeous waitress hovering above him.

"What can I get you guys?" She asked the group using one of the many smiling techniques taught to her at the Lucy Lawless School of Acting. Obviously the school was paying off; after all, it did help her acquire this gig that she was presently working on. And by the look on Adam's face, she was doing a hell of a fucking good job.

"Do you have a menu?" Adam thought that was funny, but apparently the acting school hadn't yet taught laughing or personality; regardless, the smile she was displaying would have never gotten her a passing grade. "I was just kidding. I know this fancy place doesn't have any menus. Shit, you guys don't even have a bar. I don't even see a bartender. Frankly I don't trust you posh fucks, so why don't you bring over a bottle of your best vodka, some cranberry juice, a bucket of ice, some glasses and nachos. Shush, before you say anything, I want to tell you something. I want to let you know that I have faith in you. I know that you will come back with these such items that I have requested. Come on, give me your best smile." She sort of smiled, kind of, but, yeah I guess it was a smile. Sure, she smiled. "Thank you. Here you go." Adam gave her a hundred bucks. The waitress grabbed the money and walked away. But before she could get out of sight, Adam yelled out, "And don't fucking politic about it either!"

The other three looked over at Adam in astonishment. Milay was shocked, Stacey was turned on and Chris was proud.

"Fuck yeah man!" Chris yelled at Adam and gave him a high five. "Dude, that was awesome. That's how we all need to act. Like rich douche bag fucks. You know why? That's right, 'cause tonight we are." Chris couldn't have said it any more queer.

"Yes Chris but wouldn't that just make us like one of them?"

"Fuck yeah dude that's the whole premise behind this evening. When do you ever get to do any of this bullshit? I've waited a long fucking time for this day to come. Even if after today I end up in the dumps, at least for one night I was able to be carefree. I mean completely carefree. I know you've never been able to experience that either." Chris looked around the room and then looked at Adam. "For once dude, we can tell these fucks whatever we'd like to their faces and not have to fight. I like fighting, but I'm getting a little tired of getting in trouble. Rich people hardly ever get in trouble and when they do they get off scot-free. I want that careless feeling and confidence for at least one night; and tonight is that night."

Chris stood there, panting almost; he was breathing so hard. The blood in his body had rushed to his face, not really giving him a blushing look, but instead it just produced immense veins to protrude from his forehead and neck.

"Chris, we don't have a million bucks or even ten grand, we only have a couple of thousand that we need to blow. A lot of these people here wipe their asses with the amount of cash that we have on us. We're not shit. We're less than shit, before we found this loot; we were less than the corn that's found in shit. So we can act like we have some money, but we can't act like the rest of these assholes. They're a complete different game." Adam, wise he is.

"You know what Adam, you fucking suck donkey balls. Here I am in my own happy utopian little world and you come in like Hitler into France and just fuck shit up." Chris rose his glass to Adam. "Cheers, bitch."

Milay and Stacey both just looked at each other while Adam and Chris boasted in their own magnificence. They had discussions that led to nowhere and arguments that ended as soon as one of them had the need to go to the bathroom. The night was as much pointless as it was meaningful, for it was a taste of crack cocaine for a couple of virgins of the drug scene. Adam and Chris had just both tasted a little bit of the high life, the good stuff, and they handled themselves like adults. Actually they handled themselves, more than just adults, like two men whom were accustomed to living this kind of lifestyle. They were used to living like the type of men that they both despised within a couple of hours.

"This right here Milay is why there are no good men in the world," Chris was as drunk and philosophical as ever, "men like Adam and me, all we do is bitch and complain. We complain about mother fuckers having more than us, we complain about those rich fucks not caring about the rest of us. But, as soon as we have a little taste of what they have, we understand. We understand just how selfish we humans actually are, because right now I have two words for the poor, the same poor that I will be a part of tomorrow morning. Those two words are "Fuck You". It's as simple as that. Right now I don't give a fuck that they don't have the money to be sitting in the place that I am, and I truly do not pity them for not having a girl like you with them. What could a rich man do to make the world a better place? Maybe give his money away?" Adam was too busy touching and flirting with Stacey to hear Chris's rant. "No, the best thing that a rich man could do to make the world a better place is kill himself. If he kills himself, than there is no one for the poor to be mad at. Well maybe the less poor. You know what?"

"What's that Chris?" Milay was actually listening.

"Fuck that shit. You're hot." Chris moved in closer to Milay. His thoughts and ideologies did not blend in well with booze and hormones. A good man might be able to part the two and keep himself under control, but a wise man knows to enjoy the finer things in life. At this particular moment in time, Adam and Chris were the wisest men in the world. They could care less about the world's misfortunes and focused only on their success for the night.

Motivation is what man needs to succeed and progress. Motivation comes in many shapes and forms. A politician is motivated by power, a young man by lust, an artist by alcohol, but the largest misconception is that the greatest motivator is love. Love doesn't motivate, it's the hate that love brings that fuels a person to want to succeed. Some primate hated the heat, so he got the fuck out of Africa; another hated his rival to mate, so he invented the weapon. Some hated their meaningless lives, so they created religion, while others decided to conquer. Hate drove the pilgrims to come to America. Hate drove John Starks to dunk on the Bulls. The hate of losing a loved one motivates man to seek cures. Hate drove the USA to send a man to the moon. Hate drives a rich man to become richer, a powerful man to become more powerful and so on and so on. The satisfaction of a successful goal motivated by hate is by far the sweetest.

Both Adam and Chris hated to be broke; therefore, the satisfaction that they both were currently feeling was wonderful. This night was complete for the pair of satisfied fools. They would drink, party and go home, each with a lovely woman. It was the weirdest and most eventful night of their lives, but it was soon to become just the first of many more to come. Adam Stockton and Chris Gomez would soon be the most popular and influential men in the country, two things that they were never motivated to become, for those were the two things that Adam and Chris hated more than anything. Even slackers are motivated by something, and in this case it was their hate of success.

Whatever that fucking means.

Too Good To be True

Nadaju was very happy with the way that Adam and Chris were dealing with the sporadic events occurring in their lives. The feedback being received by the production company was overwhelming. At this point, Mr. Nadaju began to sell his product to local television stations. The show was a hit in every single market that it was viewable; but now, it was time to make the transition to the US market. It's all about consumerism and who consumes more than us Americans? Nadaju would be walking around with a perpetual hard-on for a while, just as long as Adam and Chris continued their righteous ways of drinking and cursing. The hard-on would probably subside a bit if he paid more attention to the pills he was taking.

Mr. Nadaju was a prick of a man. He was pompous, pretentious, arrogant, and every other word that can be found in Roget's Thesaurus under those fore-mentioned ones. He had especially been a prick to his cleaning lady, Lupe, who he sexually harassed on a constant basis. She eventually got fed up and switched his ulcer medication with his penis medication. Although very content with the progress of the program, Nadaju had been nervous about the transition over to American television. This made his ulcer flare, causing him to take his pills, causing him to walk around with a hard-on all day long.

Its funny how one can forgets the pain of an ulcer when there is a greater pain in his penis. Speaking of dicks, let's get back to the stars of the show.

Saturday afternoon at the Stockton residence was spent watching pirated movies that he downloaded off the internet, followed by a quick nap. He woke up to a phone call from Chris asking him whether he wanted to go out for a bite to eat and a drink. Adam accepted the invitation and met up with Chris at a local dive bar. They both chatted away about the previous night reminiscing every detail and moment while they ate their greasy burgers and downed some beers. In midst of drunken screams at the TV screens and loud bustle over the juke box, which actually had a decent selection of music, Chris and Adam began to think about how truly strange the previous night had been.

"Shit just ain't right," Adam told Chris, "You know what I mean?"

"Yeah dude, I've been thinking about it all day long. That kind of shit just doesn't happen. At least not to people like us. We've been way too lucky as of lately. It's not that I mind, because I wouldn't mind having this luck for the rest of my life. It just doesn't feel right."

At that exact time, two men, who had been arguing about some lame current event factoid over by the bar, started to really get boisterous. Then, one of the men pushed the other one into the table where Adam and Chris sat. Adam, upset for having his drink spill on his lap, grabbed the man and pushed him back towards the other guy. The man that Adam pushed grabbed a bottle and threw it towards Adam nearly hitting him. The bottle smashed against the wall next to Adam's back. Chris jumped up, ran and shoulder tackled the man. The guy that the other brawling man was arguing with starts to go after Chris, but just before he could lay his hands on him, Adam caught him with a straight punch to the temple, knocking the man down and stunned him. Chris was still on the ground wrestling with the other guy, when flashing lights started to shine in from outside the bar. The bartender, knowing Chris as a regular, picked him up off the other guy and shoved Adam and him towards the back of the bar and out a door into an alley.

Adam had grabbed Chris by the shoulders and shook him while talking to him, "You see! That's what I'm talking about. We have too

Joe A. Melendez

much luck." He then let go and began to run down the alley towards the street.

As they were jogging, Chris asked Adam, "How are we too lucky? We're running down a dark alley in the middle of the night after being tossed out of a bar after being in a brawl."

"First of all, we got tossed away from the cops...."

"I know the bartender" Chris instantly rebutted.

"And secondly, we never got hit. Answer me this, when was the last time that you were in a brawl and you didn't get hit?"

"Well that's because we're getting good at it. It's only a matter of practice."

"Dude, that's bullshit and you know it. It's just too lucky."

"I agree that we've been having good luck lately, but this time was just coincidence." Chris finished his statement just as they got to the street. They began to walk on the sidewalk with the rest of the pedestrian traffic, and just like everyone else, they hung their heads low. They reached the street corner and stopped to wait for the light to change. Chris then began to speak again as the light changed from red to green, "Did you call Stacey today?"

"No, did you call Milay?"

"No, I didn't feel like hanging out with her tonight."

"Yeah, I didn't feel like hanging out with Stacey tonight, either. I think it all has to do with the too much good luck thing."

"Yeah I know what you mean. You know, you used to be a lot funnier before you got all this good fortune. You don't crack as many jokes anymore."

"Yeah I know; I haven't felt like it. I haven't been pissed off enough. You haven't been as angry either. You usually size people up all the time."

"Is this good or bad?"

"I don't know, but I don't like it."

"Good, maybe it'll piss you off enough that you'll get your sense of humor back."

"Yeah, well you're still ugly."

Chris just ignored Adam and continued to walk down the street by his side. They went down about half a block after the end of their conversation and Adam's cell phone began to ring.

"Hey Adam, it's me Stacey. You know, from last night and this morning?"

"Sorry there were a couple of Stacey's between last night and this morning, can you refresh my memory?" Adam quickly pulled Chris close to the phone, so he could hear too.

"Well, I was the one riding you like a crazy cowgirl all night long, while you licked my toes...."

Chris began shaking his head. Adam covered the microphone section of his phone so Stacey couldn't hear him speak. "No dude, I was drunk. It just seemed like the thing to do at the moment. I swear I had never done that before, the toe-licking that is." Adam then brought the phone to his ear, so Chris couldn't hear anymore.

"Oh yeah, haha, I remember. What's going on?" Adam asked.

"Oh nothing really, I was kind of hoping that you would have called me earlier to hang out tonight, but you didn't call, which is fine. I was just being...Oh I don't know, I was just being silly. I guess it's too late to hang out tonight, but how about tomorrow?"

"It's the cock, right? You can't have enough of the cock. It's a curse, I tell you." Adam looked over at Chris while he was talking to Stacey. Chris was cracking up with laughter. "I mean, it's not a curse for you. You've been blessed by the cock. But, I'm telling you, it's like crack, you're just going to crave it."

"You got me there. I could care less about you; I just want your cock. I heard that they sell home kits to make a dildo out of a mold of your cock. Maybe I should just buy you that, you make me a copy of your blessed cock and I'll see you when I see you."

"You couldn't do that. That's like substituting crack with caffeine. It gets you high, but it doesn't fuck your shit up."

Chris gave Adam a thumbs up on his last remark.

"Regardless, I'm down to hang out tomorrow. How about I give you a call around noon and we'll set something up then?"

"Sounds good to me. Talk to you tomorrow. Bye."

Joe A. Melendez

"You see, I could still be funny." Adam sought Chris's approval.

"It was alright, but it didn't seem witty enough. It sounded a little thought out, as if you had used it before."

"So what if I have? It's still good."

"Bah, whatever." Chris just shrugged off the conversation. "I'm bored, what's there to do?"

Adam just simply ignored him and continued walking for about a block and walked into a bar, sat down and ordered a beer. Chris did the same. Then finally, Adam answered Chris's question. "I don't know man. There's still some money left over. Actually, there's a decent amount of cash left over. It's one of those adverse affects of being used to always being broke. When you have cash all of a sudden, you don't even spend it. Well, we did spend like two grand."

"Yo, last night, Milay was telling me that she wants to go to the track. You know, the horse track." Chris spoke as if he were talking to his beer mug, looking directly into it.

"That's not a bad idea. Is the track open tomorrow?"

"Why wouldn't it be?"

"I don't know, because it's Sunday and gambling is like a sin and shit, so people should be in church and not sinning."

"Fuck that, god is the biggest gambler of all time. He threw us all on this earth, gave us Jesus, Muhammad, Buddha and all those other fuckers; he had us chose teams and then duke it out. He's just betting on which one of us kills who next." Chris explained.

"Yeah cool, that's great. So are you down to go to the track tomorrow?" Adam couldn't care less about myths.

"Yeah, but aren't you supposed to hang out with Stacey?"

"I'll invite her to come with us, that way she thinks I'm thinking about her and being sweet for inviting her when really all I want to do is keep banging this broad for as long as I can, because this girl is retarded hot."

"Yeah she is." Chris continued to talk directly into his beer.

They hung out at that bar for about an hour or so, playing darts, drinking beer, and just shooting the shit. At around two AM they decided to head to their designated homes.

Chris woke up early the next morning. He went through his daily routine of stretching aggressively on his bed done in conjunction with excessive swearing, nut grabbing and farting. Then he got up, walked over to his computer and checked his email. He sifted through all the spam and junk mail and finally realized that no one ever emails him, so he decided to look at some porn. He refused to look at the news anymore, since all it did was give him heartburn. The search for porn didn't last long; Chris realized that he had already seen all the porn there was to see on the internet. He got up from his desk, walked over to the kitchen and poured himself a bowl of corn flakes and milk. He walked it over to the coffee table, sat the bowl on it and walked away. He then began doing his morning exercises that consisted of push-ups, sit- ups, pull-ups (about ten of each) and pacing around a lot. Once done, he had his bowl of cereal and went off to take a shower.

Meanwhile, Adam had woken up at roughly around the same time as Chris had. He just laid there in bed for a while, wondering whether he actually wanted to get out of bed today or not. He thought about how it was Sunday and besides his previous engagement with Stacey, whom which he had to inform of the new plans with Chris and Milay, Adam had nothing to do. He didn't worry because he knew he could easily break the plans that he had with them. Then he thought about whether he was hungry or not; and if he was, whether he was hungry enough to get out of bed just yet. Luckily, he needed to take a piss, so his decision taking fiasco quickly came to an abrupt stop. Once he got out of bed, he knew he would be up for good.

Chris got out of the shower and simply stood there for a good ten minutes, he allowed himself to air dry. What ever water was left on his body he just shook it off like a wet dog. He brushed his teeth, rinsed and wiped his mouth. Then he headed back to the living room without putting on pants or even grabbing a towel to wrap his ass in. Chris didn't care that the window shades were wide open and that people in the apartment buildings across from his could just look in. He walked over to his couch and sat down, his balls flopping down on the cushion like a walrus on a beach. Chris turned the television set on and began to change the channels. He didn't even try to see what was on. He just simply changed the channels, a split second of each channel could easily expose to him what the nature of the program was and whether he wanted to watch it or not. Today being a Sunday, all there was were infomercials, Sunday mass, news reports and the kind of sports that people actually like to watch. He scanned them all.

Click, click, click, click, click……...

And so on and so on for about twenty minutes.

He scanned through all the channels at least fifty times over. All he paused on were the Spanish channels that had shows with half naked olive skinned girls dancing by gyrating every inch of their bodies on the beach. He would watch these until a commercial came on, then he would continue his surfing until he would eventually come back to the same channel when the commercials were over. After ten minutes of watching tanned girls shaking their asses, Chris was reminded of Milay. However, just before he was to get up and walk over to the phone to call her, his phone rang. He walked over to it and picked it up.

It was Milay.

Adam had been standing in his kitchen for the past fifteen minutes, scratching his belly, looking inside of the cupboards. He would open them, shut them, open them, and shut them. Eventually, he realized that he had no food to eat. The food that occupied the cupboards were reminiscent of the time that he went grocery shopping after smoking some crazy weed that one of his old college buddies had mailed to him straight from Vancouver. He had jars of peanut butter and all types of other things that Adam was allergic to. He would have thrown them out at that particular moment, but he figured that completely empty cupboards would be much more pathetic than sticking to his present collection. Adam then checked out his refrigerator. He found two-day old cold pizza and a new container of orange juice. Breakfast was served.

Just as soon as Adam had gotten comfortable on his couch, with his meal neatly placed before him on his coffee table, his phone rang. He got up and walked over to the charging dock, but his phone wasn't there. He could hear it ringing, but he couldn't quite figure out from where. He searched inside the cushions of his couch and even underneath it. He went into his bedroom and searched under his bed and amongst the clothes on his floor. The phone continued to ring. He decided to stand in the center of his living room, close his eyes and follow the sound of the ringing. He walked over to the kitchen. Stood in the center of the room and listened for the ring. He heard it coming from behind him. He searched on the counter and then began opening the cupboards. He saw the flashing of the phone as it rang. It was hidden behind the jars of peanut butter that he never ate. He grabbed the phone and pressed the answer button. As soon as he did, his phone went dead. He placed his phone on its charger and sat down to eat his breakfast. He turned the television on, surfed the channels and stopped to watch tanned Spanish girls dancing in Miami in front of a Mariachi band.

Chris had gotten off the phone with Milay and had been trying to get in touch with Adam to inform him of the plans for the day. Since he couldn't, he simply left Adam a message on his voice-mail instructing Adam to call him back. He then turned the television back on and continued to watch the Spanish girls dancing. As soon as the show was over, Chris's phone began to ring. It was Adam returning his call.

"Yo dude, what's up?" Adam spoke with a yawn.

"Nothing much man, I just called to see it you were still down for today."

"Yeah, I'm down. I just have to call Stacey and let her know of the plans."

"True, did you just wake up?"

"No man, I've been up for a while. I heard my phone ring the first time; I just didn't get to it on time and then the battery died. I've just been watching the Spanish channel since."

"Dope Spanish bitches dancing?"

"Dope Spanish bitches dancing." Adam repeated

Although, they couldn't see each other, both were nodding in agreement with each other while sporting the same stupid grins. Then both began day dreaming of the show which they had watched. Chris was the first to snap out of it.

"Yo, I talked to Milay. She says she's down to go. So, you should call Stacey up right now and set things up with her."

"Will do, I'll call you in a minute."

Adam hung up with Chris and called up Stacey. He ran the plans through her and she was as eager as a schoolgirl on a cocaine and American Idol binge. To top it off, Stacey had a car that they could use, instead of having to take the train and then a taxi. Adam told her to get ready as soon as possible and to come right over to his apartment. He then told Chris to get ready and to call and tell Milay to get ready. Then they'll go pick them up. Chris agreed.

Stacey got to Adam's apartment rather quickly. He barely had gotten himself ready before she was ringing the intercom from downstairs. He quickly got himself together and went down to meet her. He gave her a kiss at the vestibule and walked her outside. Adam complimented her on her appearance and then asked for her to show him her car.

"It's right there." Stacey pointed out.

"Oh cool." Adam walked out unto the sidewalk in order to get into the passenger side door. He walked towards a white Honda Civic and stopped.

"Why are you stopping there? It's the car in front of that one." Stacey corrected Adam.

Adam didn't budge; he simply stood there, staring at the car, and then back at Stacey, the car and then Stacey. She simply shook her head to point out that the one that he was staring at was really hers. She took out her keys and hit the button that opened the doors and started the car. Adam was still in shock.

"You drive around in a BMW?" He said.

"Yes, so what?" Stacey seemed puzzled.

"It's not the fact that you drive a BMW. It's the fact that this was a 760LI; this car is top of the line. This shit is the real fucking deal."

"Don't worry it's a company car. I couldn't afford one of these. They just lend me one for my business trips."

Adam simply got into the car and enjoyed the comforts of luxury. He gave Stacey a "thumbs up" and then told her that they needed to go pick up Chris and Milay. The short trip was pure joy for Adam; he had gotten so used to the nauseating ride of the subway and the nerve wrecking adventures of a taxi. When they got to Chris's apartment, Adam didn't even get out to ring Chris's intercom. He was much too comfortable. He simply called him up and told him to come down. Chris was down shortly. He stepped outside of his apartment building and looked around. He couldn't see into the double parked Beamer because the windows were tinted black.

You could read his lips saying, "motherfucker" for seeing no sign of Adam anywhere. Adam laughed for a minute as he watched Chris sweat outside on this muggy hot summer day. Then he told Stacey to honk the horn. Chris looked at the car but just ignored it. Stacey honked the horn several more times. Chris yelled at the car, "Shut the fuck up!" So, Stacey began to honk the horn even more. Chris put his arms in the air, in a questioning yet threatening gesture. Stacey, this time, placed her hand on the horn and left it there. Chris walked towards the car yelling out all sorts of obscenities. He was going to knock on the driver's side window, but before he could, it began to open. Chris looked down as he was about to start yelling at the driver and realized that it was Stacey.

"What the fuck?" Chris was shocked as he looked at her and then checked out the car. "I was about to throw a brick at the car if you would've kept honking that goddamn horn. Jesus H. Christ. This is your fucking car?"

"It's a loaner." Stacey replied.

"Works for me." Chris said as he opened the back door and stepped into the car. He said hello to Adam and then informed Stacey that Milay would be waiting for them right outside of some coffee shop, not too far down the avenue. When they got there, Milay had obviously seen the car before, because she didn't hesitate to walk out of the shop and head towards it. Chris slid over and allowed Milay to sit down. He gave her a kiss hello. She then greeted everyone else.

While admiring the wood finishing inside the car, Adam asked Stacey, "Do you know how to get there?"

"No," She said, "but the GPS navigational system will tell me." She then pressed a button on the center console and a small LCD screen flipped out. Then she asked it for directions to the race track and it gave it to her. Adam and Chris simply looked at each other in awe. To them, that was just about the coolest thing that they had ever seen in their lives. On the rest of the trip to the to the racetrack, Stacey and Milay did plenty of female chit-chatting and bonding, while Adam and Chris merely tried to keep their jaws from dropping as they checked out the car. Needless to say, the road trip to the track seemed like a minute to the guys.

The horse track was an unusual place. It can not be compared to any other place like Atlantic City, Reno or Las Vegas. You won't find a hint of the glitz and glamour that you would find in any of those "family oriented" gambling cities. The group paid their one-dollar each admission fee. As they walked in through the turnstiles, they were immediately over taken by the smell of desperation and lost hope. There were many sorry faces, sulking in their own self-deprecation, walking out of that place. Luckily for this group, those sulking bastards always had a daily race pamphlet to give out to those just coming into the track. Not surprisingly, the booze is relatively cheap at the horse-track. Scattered everywhere were all types of different characters. Especially fat greasy men carrying three cell phones, four different sports sections and wads of cash lining the glass walls where the tables stand out-looking the track.

"I love the smell of cigars, booze and lost dreams." Chris whispered into Milay's ear. He then excused himself from the group, so he could go use the bathroom. While standing, facing the urinal, taking care of his business, he overheard a couple of gambling gurus talking about a race that was about to happen soon. They spoke of a new-comer horse that was going to blow everyone away. Chris didn't know whether to take them seriously or not. Why would these guys be talking about this out loud? Maybe they were playing Chris for a sucker or maybe the fact that he was the only other person in the bathroom other than themselves made them carefree. Chris didn't look like he would be able to benefit from such advice. Most recreational gamblers don't usually bet anymore than a couple of dollars per race. Even a win won't get you much money. Chris finished his business, zippered up and walked back to his friends. He didn't even bother to wash his hands.

"Yo Adam, I need to talk to you."

Adam immediately thought that Chris had gotten into some trouble already. His stomach already began to bother him and he felt cold sweat approaching. But, calmness in Chris's voice settled him.

"How much money did you bring?"

"Why?"

"Well we came here to bet, right?"

"No, I came here to stand next to these low lives to make myself feel a little better about my self image."

"Okay great, give me your gambling money."

"No, why?"

"How much do you have? Just give it to me. Trust me." Chris stuck out his hand and nervously looked around him as if an illegal transaction was taking place.

"I have two hundred and fifty dollars. But why should I give it to you?" Adam reached into his pants for his wallet, but instead of pulling it out, he simply left his hand resting on it.

"We came here to gamble, right?" Chris asked.

Adam nodded in agreement.

"Well I have a hundred fifty bucks and a hot tip. I checked the pamphlet and this horse that's a shoe in has a forty-two to one pay off. If we put all our money together we can get a shit load of money."

"How is that horse a favorite, if the odds are against him forty-two to one?"

"Dude, I have my sources."

"What's the name of the horse?"

"What does it matter?"

"It fucking matters to my two hundred and fifty dollars. Now tell me."

"It's Luck B. Alady"

"Okay. I'm in." Adam was instantly sold. He handed Chris the money without even asking him anymore questions about the horse or his sources. Chris immediately placed four hundred dollars on Luck B. Alady to win. He came back with the ticket in hand, very securely grasped. That was the last of the found money. Technically, they weren't going to lose any money if the horse didn't win. Nevertheless, their nerves were shot. The horse was about to race next. They decided to get some drinks first and then head down towards the track. The girls decided that they would stay inside, because it was too muggy outside. They didn't know about the bet that was just placed.

Adam and Chris stood outside leaning on the track barrier. Chris held tightly to the ticket inside of his pant's pocket. The horns played and the horses were let free to race. Luck B. Alady was on the second to inside track. She got off to a normal start. It was nothing spectacular as she turned the first turn, but as soon as she hit the first straight away, she exploded on the track. Luck B. Alady was leaving every other horse in the dust. Then she came to the second turn and slowed down a bit; some of the other horses began to catch up until she came out to the second straight-away. She exploded once again and easily won the race by the length of two horses.

Milay and Stacey watched through the glass as Adam and Chris jumped straight up into the air and hugged each other. They could even see tears running down their faces. The guys spilled their drinks all over the place as they celebrated. Then they straightened themselves out and walked back into the inside betting area.

"Big winners, huh?" Milay asked the guys, but they couldn't answer. They just smiled as they walked up to the collections booth. A special supervisor had to be present in the actual prize giving, as well as two security guards. Once, they had collected their prize, they were offered a security escort back to the car. They got into the car. They had been at the track for less than twenty-five minutes and made just over sixteen thousand dollars. They weren't taxed because this is fiction. Stacey drove them all back to Adam's apartment. On the ride back, Stacey and Milay asked many questions, but neither Adam nor Chris could answer. They were just silent.

They arrived to the apartment in what had seemed to the guys an eternity. Once again, the four would sit around the table looking at a decent sum of unearned cash. The guys split the earnings right down the middle. This time they weren't thinking of spending it all at once. This time they didn't even know what to do. They decided to call out sick form work the next day. They would need some time to think about their new found cash. The rest of that Sunday was boring in comparison to the short time spent at the horse-track. They ordered Chinese food; Chris told everyone the story of how he received the tip and then they all went off to their respected homes. Neither of the guys had asked the girls to spend the night with them. It was a mixture of their lack of total trust towards them and their urge to roll around naked on a pile of cash, "Indecent Proposal" style.

All the World's a Stage

Nadaju was exuberant with the path that the show was taking. Viewer participation was increasing steadily. The international success was more than enough to convince American television executives to sign the show to their network. It was to be this coming season's "Prime Time" hit. It would be facing shows of roommates and retards coexisting in s sitcom world environment with a very strong and powerful cult-like following. Nadaju was every bit convinced that his show would hit viewers harder than his erect penis as he just ran into the table with it. "Fuck!"

The next day after the track experience, Adam called Chris at roughly around 9:30am. The two would have normally already been at work by this time; but, considering their previous day's blessings, they both called out. Adam had to call Chris a couple of times before he picked up the phone. Chris was ignoring the ringing in fear that it was his job calling. He always told himself, "Good luck should always be rewarded with responsibilities." Nevertheless, the ringing had finally annoyed Chris into picking up his phone.

"WHAT!" He yelled at the defenseless machine. Adam had to pull the phone from his ear to let the ringing settle. Once again, Chris yelled, "WHAT!" Luckily, Adam hadn't yet put the receiver to his ear.

"Dude, it's me." Adam finally answered.

"WHAT!" Chris yelled again.

"Douchebag." Adam replied as he put his shoes on.

"You want to go get breakfast and spend money?" Adam asked him as he juggled to put his jacket on without letting go off the phone.

"Sure, let me just finish my beer and I'll meet you at the bagel joint on the corner of Empire and Evil. Peace." Chris took a toke from his pipe, finished his beer, put on a hat, some pants and the best smelling shirt he could find and walked out the door. Adam was already half way there.

Twenty minutes after Adam got to the bagel place, Chris arrived. Adam had already had his breakfast and was just sitting there reading the newspaper. Chris said "hello" to Adam and then went to order his food. After getting all his stuff, he sat down across from Adam. He ate his breakfast and drank his orange juice while Adam read his paper. They didn't speak throughout the entire time. Chris finally finished eating and spoke, "Sorry I'm late, I got caught up."

Adam gave him a confused look and spoke back, "You live a block away."

"Yeah," Chris took a sip of his juice, "but, those Spanish broads were on TV dancing again. It's like they're always on my TV now. It's like that blue light from an electric bug zapper, it just draws me in."

"Yeah, those girls are hot. That's why I can't turn the TV on in the mornings. I'll end up wasting an hour watching garbage." Adam put his paper down as he finished the sentence and caught a glimpse of some Asian guy coming towards them from behind where Chris was sitting. The man seemed overly excited and happy and was pointing at Chris and Adam. When he got to their table, he grabbed Adam's hand and shook it and then grabbed Chris's hand to shake.

With a great big smile, he said with a thick accent, "You guys ah flucking glate! I," before he could finish what he was saying, two large men that were sitting at the next table, grabbed him and took him out of the shop. Adam and Chris looked at each other with confused looks.

"What the fuck was that about?" Chris asked.

"I've no fucking clue. Maybe he saw us at the track yesterday, when we won all that cash, or maybe he's on that crack cocaine that the kids are smoking these days."

"Whatever he is, those dudes that took him outside were fucking big. Where the fuck did they come from?" Chris turned around to see if he could catch another glimpse of the guys, but they were long gone. He turned around and shrugged his shoulders. Adam shrugged his own in response.

"So Chris, now that you are a thousandaire. What do you plan to do?"

"I'll tell you what I'm going to do, Adam." There was a slight pause by Chris so he could catch his breath. "I'm going to do nothing with it. I'll put most of it into a savings account and the rest in my pocket. I'll buy booze when I want, or maybe go to the movies. Maybe, I'll buy a new TV and a DVD player, or maybe a mountain bike, to get around. I really haven't given it much thought. How about you?"

"I'm going to pay back some bills and student loans that I've collected over the past couple of years. I need to get those monkeys off my back for once. Maybe by doing so, I won't be so pissed off every-time I go to work. I can't stand going to work, and hating my job and knowing that in the end, all that money, that I suffer for, goes directly to those fuckers that promised me better things if I went to their school. Fuck them. I'm giving them their money and telling them to go fuck themselves, but not yet. I still need like another sixty thousand bucks to be able to do that."

"And they said I was an idiot for going to City College. At least I go for free."

"Speaking of which, don't you have classes to go to?"

"I believe we're on break or something like that. I may need to register or maybe I'm done already. Either way, there's no rush, now that I hit it big."

"Chris, you're going to be broke in less than a month and then what will you do? You're not going to be able to leave that cash in a savings account without touching it."

Chris began to chuckle, "Investments dude, investments. I've got it all planned out. I've got a deal with my buddy Chico. I'm going to spot him about five grand; he will then invest that money into pharmaceuticals, doubling my money. I don't have to do anything but spot him the cash and I get ten grand in return. It's not like it's heroin or coke, so I don't feel too bad about getting some kids high. Hey and until the government intervenes, it's still a free market. How do you think the politicians get rich? They have Chicos all over the world doubling their money on other people's expenses."

Adam lights a cigarette and instantly Chris knocks it off Adam's lips. "What the fuck was that for?" Adam stared with a bit of anger in his eyes.

"You can't smoke in here, it's against the law. Now let's get out of here and push a pregnant minority down the stairs somewhere."

"Sounds like a plan to me, lets go do that, after I finish my cigarette." Adam picked up his already lit cigarette and, smoked about a third of it before putting it out in his drink. They both exited unto the street, heading in no particular direction, they just walked. People walked by, some bumped into them, others got out of their way. Chris and Adam crossed streets without ever looking at the light, no car honked at them; none even got near to hitting them. They walked for blocks and hours without a destination. They only stop periodically to have a shish-ka-bob or a hot-dog. They ignored the world on this day. The streets could have been littered with pregnant ethnic ladies hovering over dangerous stairs, they wouldn't have noticed. The crowds opened to them; no rules or laws pertained to what was important to them. That importance merely lied in their first true taste of freedom.

At the time it seemed logical, that the world might actually be changing for the better. It was changing towards a society where men like Adam and Chris could walk the streets freely with no ill intentions in their heads or worries hovering above them. It was good, nice and peaceful all wrapped up into one. It was short of being caught in a fresh milk flood as it rained chocolate chip cookies. It was not the money or the women that had come into their lives; it was the fact that they were not presently receiving phone calls from debt collectors or angry girlfriends. If they needed something, they could buy it. If they wanted to have sex with a beautiful girl, they could do so and they could do all this without fear of any laws or consequences. Mother fucking awesome.

Just Ruthless

"The Rat Race" no longer appealed to Pierre Nadaju as a proper name for his show. He wanted something edgy and mean. Something that would emphasize what Adam and Chris were all about, well at least in his eyes. One morning, while waiting on line at his local Starbuck's he overhead two young men talking about the show and one of the men said, "Yo, that show is funny. Those two dudes are just fucking ruthless." That stuck in his mind all day and night and finally decided that he came up with the great idea to call Adam and Chris's show, "Just Ruthless" in honor of its new cynical format of Nadaju still had a hard-on going strong, by the way.

The next day both Adam and Chris made it to work on time, neither one of their bosses mentioned their absence from the previous day. It actually was the first mundane day that they've had in quite a while, up until lunchtime. At 10:30am Adam had received a phone call from Stacey. She had told him that Milay, Chris and her were going to meet up for lunch and that he should come. Adam, not having any previous wondrous plans other than having the crispy buffalo-wings at the cafeteria, agreed. Chris passed by Adam's cubicle at around a quarter to noon. They did their secret handshake to make sure that neither one was an imposter. They both failed miserably, so they decided that everything was cool.

They met up with Milay and Stacey at a nice Italian restaurant. The girls were sitting in the back, near the kitchen. They waived Adam and Chris over as soon as they walked in through the door. Once again, both Milay and Stacey were looking like a pair of supermodels that had just come off the run way.

"You girls look so good that you make ugly guys like us look better." said Adam.

The girls laughed briefly before Stacey spoke, "I ordered some appetizers and a nice bottle of white wine. I hope you guys don't mind."

Chris said, "The least amount of decisions that I need to make, the better."

Shortly after the guys sat down, the waiter had brought over the bottle of wine, followed by the appetizers. They were all chatting senselessly, talking about things that no one cared about. It was the type of conversation that Adam and Chris only cared about because it was coming out of the mouths of some very attractive women. For all they knew the girls could have been talking about the French revolution; it didn't matter because they sure were hot. They had just ordered their entrées when Milay began to tell the group a story about her father and how she believes that he is "connected". She told them stories about her father's shady friends, how they never had real jobs and how they were always loaded with money. Then she began to cry, telling the group how worried she was for him because she thought he might be in trouble with some heavy hitting guys.

Chris looked extremely bothered; he didn't know how to cope with the whole situation. He didn't want to seem like a tough guy and ask her what he could do to help and he didn't want to be a sensitive guy and ask her what he could do to help. So he just sat there and ate his lunch. Stacey leaned over to comfort her, and then they both excused themselves to go freshen up. As they walked towards the bathroom, two mountains of muscle shaped in the form of two goombas came running through the front door straight through the dining area and snatched Milay and Stacey. They took them right through the kitchen and right out the back door. It took no longer than half a minute. The other people in the restaurant were frightened and screamed. Adam and Chris were the only two in the whole restaurant that were not saying anything. They just sat there and ate their food.

Adam looked over to Chris. Chris refused to look up from his plate. Adam just kept staring at Chris. Every second, Adam's jaw would drop a centimeter more. Finally, Chris put his fork down and with out looking up from his plate, he began to speak, "That didn't just happen. They'll be back from the bathroom anytime now. You just wait my friend. Any second now." Adam closed his mouth, nodded in agreement and sat back on his chair. He stared off at the bewildered patrons of the restaurant who were looking back at them; he nodded his head in agreement once more, but this time to the patrons. He looked back at Chris, Chris finally looked at Adam and they both nodded their heads to each other.

"This is bad....Real bad." Chris said. "What the hell happened? What can we do about this?"

"How the fuck should I know? I was going to eat crispy buffalo-wings today; instead I decide to come here and be witness to a kidnapping. I could have been eating buffalo-wings!" Adam was clearly angry, as witnessed by nearly twenty people in that restaurant. "I didn't know Milay was Italian, I thought she was Chinese or something, Philipino maybe."

"Fuck, I thought she was Cuban. What kind of name is Milay?"

It only took a matter of three minutes for the police to arrive at the restaurant. They began to question everyone especially Adam and Chris. They asked the two what they had seen, if they recognized the guys, and if there was anything weird going on. Adam and Chris both told the police the story that Milay had been telling them about her father being "connected" and in trouble. The police took down their statements and their information and told them that they could go but they would be in touch with them shortly. Adam and Chris decided that this whole fiasco was too much too handle to go back to work. So, they decided to grab a bottle of Jim Beam and head back to Adam's apartment.

Chris cracked open the bottle as soon as he walked into the apartment building and began to chug. Adam would then grab the bottle and chug himself. They both dropped immediately onto the sofa as they walked into the room. Adam took out the little box from under his table and pulled out a glass pipe and a bag of weed. He began to pack it and smoke it, handing it to Chris between puffs. They didn't talk about what had just happened at the restaurant; instead they got wasted and watched the television. They both passed out shortly. Chris woke up a couple of hours later still a little drunk. He had awoken to the sound of Adam dropping the toilet seat onto the porcelain. He looked at his watch and it said ten-thirty. He got up and told Adam that he was going to head home. Adam was only pissing while sleepwalking, and when he was done, walked passed Chris straight into his bedroom; where he plopped onto his bed.

Chris staggered down the stairs and out the door. He decided that the best thing to do was walk home so that he could sober up. He had walked a couple of blocks when he decided to go through less busy avenues. He turned the corner to a less crowded street and almost immediately saw the flashing lights and heard that stupid noise that cops can make with the toys in their vehicle. He looked over to his left to see a couple of detectives waiving him over. Chris yelled over to them, "Dude, I'm not wasted. Yes I've been drinking, but I'm mostly sober right now and I'm heading home. I'm going straight home. I promise I won't cause any problems. You can follow me if you want."

"Just come over here already! We need to talk to you!" The Cop yelled back.

Chris walked over there, leaned over and asked, "What?"

The Cop in the passenger seat began to speak. "How you doing, Chris? A little wasted? What's the matter, you needed to get fucked up to forget about something? What you do, that you need to forget about so quickly?"

"What the fuck are you talking about?" Chris recognized the driver as one of the detectives that had questioned him earlier. "Dude, you were there. They kidnapped my girlfriend and her friend right next to me. That's what I needed to forget."

"Yeah, it's real funny how everyone in the restaurant said that you didn't even budge when it happened, that you looked cool as a cucumber and even continued to eat. Get in the car Chris."

"Fuck No."

"Get in the car or we'll wait until you start running, then we'll shoot you in the leg and beat you for resisting arrest. Now it's your choice."

"Cocksuckers," was the only thing that Chris said as he opened the backdoor of the cop car and got inside.

Meanwhile, Adam woke up to the sound of pounding at his front door. He tried to ignore it for a while, but it wouldn't go away, so he placed his two pillows on his head, covering his ears. This seemed to work perfectly because the noise stopped. He began to fall back to sleep until he felt two set of giant arms picking him up, gagging him and putting him in a giant duffle bag. They carried him out his door, down the stairs and out the front door. He heard them open the trunk to a car. They placed him in it and then shut it closed. He felt the car start and then drive away. At this point, the Jim Beam that he had drank a couple of hours ago seemed to be reappearing in his stomach and not agreeing with the situation. He held it in with all his might.

Fortunately, the car stopped, the two goons stepped out, opened the trunk and carried him out. Adam heard a door open, and he felt them taking him up some other stairs. Then he heard another door opening. The goons sat him on a chair, Adam was still in the duffle bag, and unzipped the bag so that Adam's face was showing.

They removed his gag and Adam simultaneously began to vomit all over the duffle bag, himself and the floor. They took him out of the duffle bag and moved him to another chair on the other side of the room. One goon stood in front of him while the other went for a mop to clean the vomit up.

Adam smiled a little bit, "Sorry about the vomit."

Meanwhile, Chris was taken to a police station and brought directly into an interrogation room. They sat him on a steel chair in front of a steel table across from the two detectives. He asked for some coffee and they brought him some. The one detective began to speak.

"Chris, so what happened today? Shit got a little weird huh?"

"Dude, I already told you what happened." Chris said in between his sips of coffee. "This is some pretty good coffee. What is it hazelnut?"

"How the fuck should I know? Just answer our questions. Isn't it a little convenient that these guys knew where to go to kidnap the girls and why were you so fucking calm? It's like you knew what was going to happen." The detective was now standing over Chris.

"Do I look calm now, Detective? If I do, it's because I knew all this shit was going to happen. As soon as I saw the girls get kidnapped I knew what was happening next."

"What the fuck do you mean? What are you talking about?" The Detective seemed a little confused and worried. Chris noticed the detective getting worried and became a little suspicious. Chris began to look around the room.

"What the fuck is going on here?" Chris asked.

"You tell me Chris. You seem to know what's going on here." The Detective seemed to gain a little bit more confidence.

"What I meant with what I just said is that people like me always get taken in by the cops for shit that they didn't do. I knew as soon as they kidnapped the girls, you pigs would harass me. So I saw all this bullshit coming. The one thing that I didn't realize until now is that this whole thing is fake." Chris finished his coffee, leaned back on his chair and put his feet up on the table.

"What the hell are you talking about Chris?!" The detective said pigishly.

"You idiots, I shouldn't be able to do this." Chris leaned back further and crossed his arms.

"Cut the shit already, you're pissing me off. You shouldn't be able to do what?" The Detective oinkishly became aroused.

"First, I know this is fake and have nothing to worry about, because a real cop would have tried to scare me a lot better than you did without getting nervous. If you were someone that had intentions of hurting me and were just pretending to be cops, you would have already beaten the crap out of me. But, the one thing that told me that all this is fake is this," Chris rocked the chair back and forth, "You ever see a police station where they didn't have the interrogations chairs bolted to the floor? A chair can be used as a weapon or a shield." Chris stood up and placed the chair in front of him.

"Sit back down, before we get angry!" The detective yelled.

"Or what?" Chris picked up the chair with both arms.

"Put that down!" The two detectives began to back off.

"Okay." Chris nodded his head and then swung and threw the chair through the double-sided mirror. He was shocked to see a camera and crew behind the glass. "What the fuck is going on! Who are those fucking people? Am I being 'Punked'?!"

"Chris calm down! That's for documentation, they're FBI, kidnapping is a federal offense!" The detective yelled as he held his hands out.

"Bullshit! These hippies aren't FBI! You know what else is supposed to be nailed down? The table!" Chris grabbed the table and swung it towards the wall that stood behind him. It went right through the false wall full of sound proofing material, creating a huge hole.

Meanwhile, Adam found himself sitting in an empty apartment being stared at by two huge goons. Adam figured that if he didn't speak, the goons wouldn't get angry and beat on him. After a period of time, which felt like an eternity to Adam, one of the goons spoke, "We're waiting for our boss to show. He'll be here any minute."

"How polite of him to inform me." Adam thought. They stood around for a little while longer before Adam couldn't help but to speak, "So, you guys like your job? How are the benefits?"

One of the goons began to answer, "Not bad, we get the benefit of beating the shit out...." But before he could finish, the boss walked in to the apartment. He was a stereotypical mobster in every sense of the word. The shoes, the suit, the hat, the hair, not a thing was imperfect on this man. The only thing missing was the theme song from the Godfather, which Adam couldn't keep himself from playing in his head.

"You must be Adam. Yes?" Said the Don. Adam thought that his accent was very impressive.

"Yes, I am the one that they call Adam."

"Haha, we've got ourselves a funny one. Well Adam, how funny would it be if I cut your balls off and shove them down your throat?" Adam felt that the accent really added to the mood of this situation.

"Well not only for my sake, but also for the sake of the continuation of my people I would rather keep my balls attached exactly where they belong and operational. I promise to keep my mouth shut from now on." Adam was really hoping that the mobster was bluffing; he knew he couldn't keep his mouth shut for too long.

"Listen Adam, we have nothing against you personally, so let's keep it that way. I like you Adam, so hopefully we can help each other. You get me what I need and I let you keep your balls attached. How's that sound?" The Don finished his statement by sucking on his front teeth with his tongue.

Adam liked the thought of keeping his balls attached, "Sounds good to me. What do you need?"

"You see Adam, you're a clean cut guy, a nice looking respectable guy. We couldn't ask your friend Chris to do this because no one would take him seriously, but you Adam, people take you serious. That's why I need you. You see, Milay's father owes me some money. I really need that money to pay some bills. Do you catch my drift Adam? If I don't get that money, someone will get hurt and I swear to San Gennaro that it ain't going to be me. I need you to relay a message to Milay's father for me. I want you to tell him that Giancarlo told you to get two hundred and fifty thousand dollars from him.

You tell him he contacted you anonymously, so you can't describe his face because if you did, you would end up in some cans of tuna fish. Tell him that you will hold on to the money until we contact you back. When we get the money, he will get his daughter back" Once again he sucked his teeth when he finished talking.

"Why didn't you guys do that, contact me anonymously? I mean, you could have told me all this while I wore a blindfold or you could have left me zipped up in the duffle bag. I would have never known it was you. You could have truly been anonymous. Now, that I know who you are, what keeps you from killing me after I get your money?" Adam began to say his good-byes to his balls after he finished talking.

The Don was a little surprised, "Adam I thought I had made it clear to you that you needed to keep your mouth shut and simply agree. I do things the way I do for a damn good reason. We might turn you into tuna fish after you get our money or we might not, but at least you have a fifty-fifty chance. The way that your moving your mouth, you have a slim chance and.." but before the Don could finish saying what he needed to say he was interrupted by some yelling coming from the other side of the door.

"What the fuck is that?" Asked Adam.

"Eh, that's another guy who doesn't seem to want to keep his balls and keeps giving us a hard time." He looked at a Goon and said, "Tony go see what the fuck is going on in there, make sure everything is under control." The goon nodded and went on his way. "Well Adam, what do you have to say?"

"I say I guess I have no choice. You're the boss." Adam felt his chances might be a little better if he could first get himself out of this room alive.

The Don was about to respond when he was interrupted again, but this time by the sound of glass breaking. He asked his other goon to go check it out. He also pulled a small switchblade from his coat pocket. "In case you try to get tough because my boys are gone, think again. I'll have you sliced up faster than you can cry for Jesus himself to help you.

I'm glad that you finally decided to help me. I knew you were a smart boy." He walked towards the wall, leaned his back on it and began to pick his nails with his knife. He began to suck on his teeth again but was knocked forward by a sudden crash that came through the wall. Adam stood up and walked towards the hole.

Dumbasses

Adam peered in through the hole to see Chris looking back at him. Adam kicked the table out of the way and walked through the hole. Chris helped him unbind his hands. Adam looked through the broken double sided mirror and saw the cameramen, the crew and the two goons standing there. He looked over to Chris and asked him, "What the fuck is going on here?"

"That's what I've been trying to figure out. Dude, did you puke on yourself? That's fucking sick. Fuck, I think I'm going to be sick now." Chris was able to control his stomach from not giving way. "I think the people to ask are those douche-bags in there." Chris pointed at the crew on the other side of the broken mirror. He began to walk towards them when one of them stood up. It was a small fragile man with a bald head, a beard and wire rimmed glasses.

The man began to speak, "I am Jacque-Pierre Nadaju. I am the executive producer of this program."

"Is this like Candid Camera or Punk'd? Because I really hate those shows and I don't like to be fucked with. By the way Chris, did you do all this destruction? Good job angry one." Said Adam. Chris just nodded and smiled.

"Well, not exactly Adam. You guys have been part of a new reality show ever since you were hired to work at Hardmega Tech."

"That can't be legal, you can't just film us without us knowing, that's invasion of privacy." Adam had remembered something from one of his civics classes in college.

"Well, actually you guys did sign a contract approving of the filming. You two happened to be the only guys that didn't read any of the paper work. We even verbally told you during the interviews. I don't even know how to explain it. You guys sat through an orientation." The man just looked at the two as they looked at each other.

"Dude, I can't even remember Sunday nonetheless a couple of months ago. Adam do you remember?"

"I was high for that shit. I was just worried that you guys were going to ask me to take a drug test. Everything else seemed like bullshit. I got a question though. How come nobody ever talked about it at work? How come we never found out? This is a huge city, how is it that no one recognized us from the show?"

"There is a clause in the contract forbidding anyone that works at Hardmega Technology from talking about it. They would suffer greatly if they did, as long as they were under that contract. As for the rest of the city, it's New York City, I just saw some guy get stabbed earlier today and people simply stepped over him. No one notices shit and you guys are lucky, because you two guys are famous, huge hits all across the globe. You two have your own show called "Just Ruthless".

"So the show is about us and its called 'Just Ruthless'? I don't get it." Chris asked .

"Everyone that works with you were all candidates at some point. First we, the producers, narrowed it down to forty of you. Remember the downsizing?"

"No."

"Well whatever. Then we began to air the show and had the viewers cast an online vote. This went on for a couple of episodes until they finally voted on the two of you. They seemed to love the fact that you two were just real and, for lack of a better word, individuals. You said and did whatever you wanted as if you weren't in front of a camera. It took us a little while to figure out that you guys really didn't know you were in front of the camera. When we did, we focused on you two; and that's when our ratings sky-rocketed. You guys are going to be filthy rich."

Nadaju was full of shit. I told you before why Adam and Chris got chosen to be the main characters of "Just Ruthless". Nadaju is just trying to squirm his way out of another tight situation by laying on the grease.

"That's all nice and all, but why would you play this kidnapping prank on us?" Chris said as he sat down on the only chair left standing in the room.

"You see, we assumed that once you came across some money, yes we planted the cash in the wallet and we also rigged the horse race, that you two would go wild and crazy like a couple of rock stars. We were all excited after that first night you guys went out with the girls and were hoping for some more of that. Instead, we saw the potential of you two just becoming complete slackers and we couldn't take that chance."

"So what the hell has been real and what has been fake?"

"Honestly, the only thing that is real in the show is you guys. Everything else had been arranged or choreographed. Chris, that guy you knocked out and robbed is an actor and stuntman. Stacey and Milay are both actresses and by the way we didn't force them to do anything that they didn't want to do."

"Shit, we don't care about that. Now that we're famous we can get all sorts of fake broads. They'll be coming out the woodworks, super beautiful and infatuated by our money and fame. Thanks a lot asshole." Chris stood as he finished speaking

Adam began to speak, "You made the world love us and now they're not going to leave us alone. We hate everyone. We even hate women like Milay and Stacey and if it weren't for the fact that they were the sexiest girls we have ever seen in our lives we would have completely ignored them. This is why we are pricks, because we're sick and tired of falseness. We are completely honest all of the time, while everything else around us is fake. This reality show couldn't be any more real. It shows the world how fake the world really is. If we were normal than it wouldn't be entertaining and all that we are is honest." Adam looked over at Chris, "Chris do it."

Chris picked up the chair and threw it back through the broken mirror hitting and breaking the camera. They began to walk out as everyone just watched, but before they left Chris yelled, "We still better get our money douchebags!"

Nadaju had wanted to stir up the lives of Adam and Chris a bit in order to ensure high ratings. He was determined to make "Just Ruthless" into the biggest show on the face of the earth. Chris's actions were unexpected to Nadaju, but he knew something good when he saw it. He decided to show the episode, unedited, censored only for adult language, of course the raw footage was to be made available all over the internet. "Just Ruthless" was truly a success. It WOULD be the most watched program on the planet, but it would also make Adam Stockton and Chris Gomez the most influential beings on Earth.

The world was fucked.

The Truth was Out

"What the fuck was that all about?" asked Adam. Chris was just shaking his head and trying to stay as far from him as possible, seeing that Adam was covered with puke and all.

"That was retarded." Chris said and followed it by spitting a huge wad of phlegm on to the wall. "So, we're on TV. Are we celebrities or something?"

"This is going to suck ass. Could you imagine how many people are going to come and piss us off?" Adam said, wiping some puke off his chin.

"Dude, do you know how much pussy we're going to get?" Chris looked over and smiled at Adam after he finished saying it. Adam smiled, exposing some remnants of something that he once had deep inside of him and had resurrected 3 days later, like Jesus, and was now crucified, once again like Jesus, between Adam's two front teeth, not like Jesus. Chris looked away in disgust and they both continued towards the exit door.

Adam and Chris left the building knowing that their lives had changed forever. They didn't know what to do with themselves. Their hearts were pumping too fast to go home and go to sleep and their stomachs were too turned to go to a bar and drink, but they were willing to go and give it a try. They walked around for a little while, trying to find a "safe" bar, one that wouldn't involve fresh plot twists to "up" the ratings. They couldn't do it. Their paranoia was far too overwhelming for them to handle. They both needed to run and so they did.

They ran straight for the train station. The whole time Chris was sputtering random obscenities, spitting and kicking garbage cans. "They can't air this shit on network TV!" he would yell. It was late night or early morning in the city, so a scene like this is common. People had gotten accustomed to the insane crack heads barking at the televisions behind the store windows, accusing the cameras of espionage. They might actually not be so crazy, come to think about it.

They both jumped the turnstiles and made it over to the train in time to catch it. They easily found two empty seats, considering the whole train was empty. There, sat two guys, side-by-side, staring down to the ground; both of them, dirty and smelly in their own very unique ways. Chris looked over at Adam, "Where to man? What the fuck do we do now? Do we continue living our lives and ignore the fact that we're celebrities on a hit television show or do we end it? I don't mean kill ourselves, I mean we should see if we can get out of this show thing."

Adam looked up over to Chris, "Ummmm." He drew it out for quite awhile. "The past couple of weeks have been a lot of fun, especially the past couple of days. I say we go along with it all for a bit. We make some cash. This shit will eventually be cancelled. We disappear from sight and the whole world will simply forget about us. Someday we might be broke and do some "Whatever Happened to Those Guys" show on us and get paid. This might be the thing that we actually needed in life, a kick-start to something great and more glorious than where our pitiful lives were taking us. I say we run with this."

Chris was shaking his head in agreement. "You're fucking right. We should definitely milk this as much as we possibly can. People will fuck with us, but it'll be fun, because then we can just fuck with them even worse. So many broads will want to bang us. We'll get free shit for product placement and more loot. Yeah man, this might be fun."

They sat back and crossed their arms, leaning their heads on the glass and regretting to do so when the train jolted and the two guys slammed their skulls into it. They sat up and collected their senses. They both decided to head to their respected homes to just chill for a bit and take the rest of the week off from going to work. They hung out at home, watched DVD's, and what ever else they could actually see. Anything that mentioned them was removed and any channel that carried them was as well. They pretty much had nothing to watch but the History channel and the shopping channels, so TV was pointless. They talked to themselves on the phone every once in a while to try and finish deciding how they were going to carry out their plan.

They decided to stay put at home and hold out till Monday, when they would return to their jobs as if everything was still normal, sort of. They would be the guys who they were and say what they always said and act how they always acted. Nothing would be different.

On Monday morning, Adam and Chris had decided to meet up at a coffee shop before going into work, this way they would arrive together at exactly the same time. (So much for keeping it normal. Dumbasses.) Surprisingly enough, they both arrived at the coffee shop at the time that they had agreed. They had their bagels and their coffee and went outside to smoke a cigarette. Then they both headed to work.

So far everything really did seem normal. "Maybe the show is a failure and no one is watching." Thought Adam. He felt a bit bummed out about that.

Adam and Chris took turns going through the revolving doors, Adam first and then Chris. Adam waited for Chris to come through before continuing forward to go through security; Chris went first followed by Adam. They both got through without a glitch and headed for the elevator, one immediately arrived to take them up to their floor, the fourteenth floor. I don't need to explain to you all why this building goes from twelve to fourteen. I hope that by now you have picked up a little bit of useless information along your own special lives.

The doors opened and they turned left, down the hall and stopped at where the office area opened up to a large room full of small grey cubicles. Adam was to head to his and Chris was to continue to walk past everyone and head to the back, where the mailroom was located. But before they did, they both looked at each other and shook hands. Then as Adam turned left to head to his little grey box, Chris jumped into the air and gave out a loud yell, "WOOOOHOOOOO!" Surprisingly enough, everyone ignored him, even Adam. Chris, disappointed, simply walked back to the mailroom while Adam sat down at his desk.

Another Day, Another Dollar

Adam was staring at his computer, simply surfing the internet, looking to see if that thing he ordered, that came in wrong, was being taken care of by now. He got stuck looking at porn and other websites created for immature men and sick fucks. Then he stumbled upon something on one of the sites. It was a photoshopped picture of Chris sucking Adam's dick. Adam was staring at it in disgust when Susan peaked over the cubicle to say "good morning" but was sidetracked by the picture on his monitor. He quickly closed the window and looked up at Susan.

"Howdy?" He asked with a stupid grin on his face.

"Howdy there cowboy, have you been riding some studs lately?" Susan was quick to respond.

"Oh no Susan, that's not what you think it was, that wasn't real." Adam had the deer stuck frozen in front of your headlights look. The same look on your face when your mom catches you cranking one out to her Victoria's Secret catalogue, reminding you that you're cranking one out to a catalogue of women's lingerie that belongs to your mother, therefore she might be wearing some of those things at this present moment, ruining the precious instance where you spew all over Adriana Lima's tight little ass.

"Don't worry Adam, I know what that was. Kenny from accounting made it, at first it was in company email, but somehow it has spread all over the internet. It was just a joke, considering that you and Chris just so happen to be out of work the same days, all the time."

"Oh great so everyone now thinks we're two big homo's that are vacationing at fire island, while we enjoy peace and tranquility away from all forms of prejudice and discrimination. Susan, I only wish that was the case." Adam was almost at the brink of tears, forgetting exactly why what he had seen on his computer was truly offensive to him. He quickly remembered. Although he was the one receiving the blowjob, thus proclaiming Chris as the bitch, it still was a picture of some dude sucking his cock. The fact, that it was fake, was beside the point.

"Okay so tell me, what have you two been up to and why haven't you been inviting me?"

Adam hadn't prepared for an array of questioning, even though this is clearly a question that Adam and Chris should have both been getting prepared to answer. They thought things wouldn't really be back to normal when they came back. Adam thought that maybe their little fiasco a week ago had changed the network's plans. Once again, Adam got smacked with the reality bat. He was now dreading the thought of actually being stuck at this menial, pointless and pathetic job. He snapped out of his small trance and decided to answer Susan's question, just as soon as he thought of an answer. And he thought, and thought and continued to think as Susan waited, her jaw dropping lower and lower with every second that past.

Then he spoke, " My foot was hurting real bad for no apparent reason so I had to go to the hospital. When I took my sock off to show the doctor, he noticed a strange red bump on the top of my foot. I never even noticed it before. He said he would take a better look at it with an x-ray. As my foot appeared to be nothing more than bone and outline on his monitor, he also saw something else. Where that bump was located was a small metal disc. He asked me some questions and I honestly didn't know where it came from. He decided that the best thing to do was to remove the object. So he did."

Susan waited patiently as Adam just looked at her calmly. She finally said something, "Then what?"

"That's it; he removed the metal disc and threw it out. Maybe, he kept it. I don't know and don't care. I didn't want it."

"So that's it? You aren't curious to what it could have been?" Susan surely was.

"Yeah, of course I was and would still be if it wasn't removed. I see all the time on TV shows about alien abductions. They always have these fuckers saying that they had a small metal disc or whatever removed from their bodies. Then they parade all over the fucking place with this little thing saying their story. Well let me tell you something, Sue. If aliens were able to implant that thing in my foot without me noticing, then maybe I should stay as far as possible from whatever they stuck in my body. And to then parade on TV is retarded.

Imagine that Susan, you escape being tracked by advanced space aliens, yet you decide to be all over the TV. You don't think Aliens have cable? Well, most likely they have satellite; them being in spaceships and all."

"I see. So what about your foot? It seems fine and what about Chris? I know you were with Chris, because there isn't a chance in hell that you two are out for exactly the same days."

"It's been more than a week for my ankle to heal and, well Chris is a fucking space alien. Who do you think could have implanted something into my foot without me noticing? He's the only one that could have gotten close enough to my foot when I was passed out. I always suspected him of being from out of space, but this whole foot tracker implant thing just proves it."

"Why would Chris implant a tracker in you, if you two are always around each other?" Susan was quick, but Adam had brought his "A" game today.

"Well, you see Susan, now you're simply answering your own questions." Adam smiled.

Susan was starting to have a hard time tracking the truth down, understandable enough considering the lack of any. "What the fuck are you talking about?"

"You really aren't paying attention. Chris is an alien who has taken human form and has come here to place a tracker on me so that his other alien buddies and him can have a good laugh or two every now and then by just tuning in. Although his human disguise is not so good, he still managed to befriend me. He forcibly got me intoxicated and implanted the tracker.

His mission being complete, he beamed back up to his ship. However, when he checked in on me a couple of days later he obviously found out that I had it removed. So he came back. And I'm back. So we're all back trying to implant tracking devices into each other. Susan, I might have to implant a little device in you and track ya."

"You're so full of shit. What the hell did you two really do?"

"Okay, fine. You want to know the truth? I kind of fell into some money; so Chris and I went to the horse track to place some bets. We won a nice chunk of change. We decided that it would be a good time to take a week off from work and go on an unexpected vacation. So we went to South Beach."

"I knew you two were gay."

Adam really wished he had chosen a lesser beacon of gay man vacationing locations. "We went with some broads so fuck you." Who's gay now? Not our manly Adam Stockton.

"Fuck you." Susan simply replied and turned around to sit back at her desk. Adam was satisfied. He turned around and continued to surf and play games on the internet. He focused on the clock waiting for lunchtime to come. It seemed to drag for the hour to come, until he got sucked into an intense game of online spades. At just the moment in which Adam was most focused, Chris walked by, peeked into Adam's cubicle, walked in and shut Adam's computer off. Adam looked up at him in amazement.

"Let's go fucker, it's lunch time. Finish your game later." Chris walked out the cubicle. Adam began to search all over his desk for something to launch at Chris's dome. He couldn't find anything decent so he got up and followed Chris. When they stopped at the elevator, Adam asked Chris what he had told people he was doing. "I was sick." Is what Chris told Adam he said. Adam sure wished he had chosen something as simple. The elevator door opened and they walked in, calm muzak played.

They both stared forward at the elevator door waiting for their descent to finish. Adam began to hum in unison with the muzak. It was some Police song performed by a xylophone-wielding robot. Chris looked over at Adam and said, "This is taking a while today."

"Yup, does seem a little slow." Adam continued to hum the tune. Chris began tapping his fingers on the wall to the beat of the song. "Is the fucking elevator even moving?" Adam asked as he began to jump up and down.

"I think so, but it's moving really fucking slow. It's getting hot in here, too." Chris stared at Adam, they both thought the same thing. "This is another one of those stupid antics created to boost ratings." The music began to get louder and sweat began to cover Chris's forehead, glistening on his veins that began to protrude. Adam was becoming very irritated as well. He looked over at Chris and nodded his head. Chris began to follow the muzak with his ears, like Mr. Miyagi following the fly with his eyes before he snatched it with chopsticks. Finally, Chris found the source of the music, a small speaker located on the ceiling of the elevator.

He pulled out his pocketknife, jumped up and jammed it well into the side of the slightly protruding disc. Chris then jumped again and smacked the butt-end of the handle even deeper in. He got tired of jumping so he told Adam to give him a boost up. Adam cupped his hands together and held them for Chris to step unto and lift himself up to the speaker. Chris had begun pulling down on the knife handle when the speaker began to give way. Adam was beginning to tire and the speaker was beginning to come off, when the elevator door opened at the lobby, exposing them to the crowd gathered waiting for their trip on the elevator. Adam dropped Chris to the ground and waved to the people. Chris put his knife away.

"The fucking thing is broken." Chris told the people. "I'm gonna need to take it in, to fix." He then jumped up and ripped the speaker down. They finally left the elevator, Chris with speaker in hand. They walked down the lobby towards the exit doors. Lavash stood guard as usual.

"Give me the speaker Chris." Adam held his hand out. Chris placed the speaker in it. "Hey Lavash, my good man, I've got something for you." Adam tossed the speaker to Lavash. Before he could even question the gift, Adam and Chris were both out of the building. Lavash could still be seen through the glass simply staring at the speaker in his hands. He shook it up to his ear and even took a

Joe A. Melendez

whiff at it. Adam and Chris simply kept walking out past view. The two headed straight for a small pizzeria, just around the corner. It was a quieter day than usual. There was less traffic on the road and less people on the sidewalks. They didn't even notice.

They got to the pizzeria to discover there was no line at all. Usually this pizzeria is packed with people, especially at this time of the day. Adam and Chris walked right up to the counter without even bumping into anyone.

"Yo, where's Tony?" Adam asked the guy behind the counter.

"Tony, ain't here today. He took the day off." Said the young guy. The guy behind the counter can be described in a couple of different ways. First of all, he's a young man; he might be in his early twenties at the oldest estimate. He is a very common breed of man in this area, your typical "guido". For those of you who are not aware what a guido is, let me go into further detail.

Although the majority are, a guido doesn't necessarily have to be, from an Italian background. They do, however, express the same lack of taste as all guidos from across the globe. The juiced up muscle physique, the "Brooklyn" spiky hair cuts, the shitty tribal tattoos, the Armani Exchange tee shirt, the BMW that daddy paid for with the CD changer full of crappy electronic music. Not all guidos are bad people, but they are definitely clueless and fun to make fun of.

"What do you mean he's not here today? He's always here, always. Did I mention that he's always here?" Adam thought that he had made a valid point, one worthy of an answer, but Chris interrupted.

"Yeah let me get two slices, and some of those garlic knots."

"How many you want, half a dozen?" The guido ignored Adam and began to cut a pie into slices and throwing them into the giant oven behind him.

"Yeah, that sounds good." Chris replied.

The guido rounded up a half dozen garlic knots, tossed them on a pan in the oven and turned to Adam. "What can I get you?"

"I'll just have two slices." Adam and Chris got their food and went back to sit at an unusually unoccupied table. They had no need for conversation, since their situation was obvious. New York City doesn't just change because it's Monday or it's a holiday or for no other reason, except money. The empty streets and pizza parlor are only empty because the show is still on. This idea, once again, brought mixed thoughts and feelings to the two stars. The perks might be nice, but will it really be worth it and how long is this whole thing going to last? They ate their lunch and walked outside.

"So what's next?" Chris asked Adam as he lit a cigarette. Adam lit a cigarette too and began to start walking. Chris followed him.

"You need to stop asking me that. I don't know what's next. We decided to ride this fucker out, so that's it. That's what's next."

"Yeah, but can we do whatever we want? Look around you, shit is obviously not normal. So why should we continue to live our lives normally? They pulled some fucked up shit on us, even though it might have gotten us laid by some really hot broads and got us a little bit of cash." Chris said as he and Adam crossed the empty street with no need to look both ways.

"To tell you the truth Chris, I really don't have the urge to do anything outrages. Yes I loved the broads and the cash, but that last stint was a real pain in the fucking ass. This is reality television, god knows what they'll be having us do next."

"So what? We can't possibly be too surprised by anything anymore. I say we just ride whatever they throw at us. How bad can it be?" Chris flicked his cigarette.

"Dude, don't say that. That's pretty fucking cliché. Something so unoriginal as that is bound to wind up on a commercial." Adam flicked his cigarette. He didn't notice the big goofy dude that blocked the cigarette's route towards the pavement. "Oh shit, my bad man. Didn't mean to burn you."

"That's alright sir." The big goofy man simply smiled at Adam and walked on past him. Adam kept on walking not even thinking twice about the man. He figured it was just another retard roaming the streets. It felt nice for Adam to walk amongst his own. He looked over at Chris and gave him an "all-gums" smile. If you're not sure what that is, walk over to a mirror and give yourself a big smile, as big as you can, but cover your top teeth with your bottom lip. If you still don't know, then you're most likely already a retard, yourself.

They walked past the lack of pedestrians on the sidewalk and continued on towards their office building. Lavash was still standing inside, perplexed, staring at the speaker given to him by Adam. Adam and Chris walked in through the doors. Chris kept walking as Adam stopped to talk to Lavash. "Yo man, it's the speaker for the elevator. It was broken, so Chris brought it down. That's it man. Call maintenance." Adam just kept looking at this giant human, waiting for a response. But, none came. Lavash simply kept fondling the speaker and wires that came out of it. "Lucky Bastard" Adam thought to himself.

He caught up with Chris by the elevator doors, waiting for an elevator to finally arrive. It did, just as soon as Adam got there. "Holy fuck man, I guess they want us to fucking stick together. You said, 'Act normal.' We couldn't even make it past lunch before shit was no longer 'normal'." They both walked into the elevator. This was a different elevator from the one that they had ridden before. This elevator's muzak was much louder and more annoying than the last. Chris began to get hot and sweaty, not because of the unusual heat that now filled the elevator or the annoying music or even the slow ascent. It was the fact that this was being deliberately done to them.

Adam tried to tune everything out. He ignored the heat, music and slow ride. He thought about how all this could ultimately benefit him and how all this will be worth it in the future. Then he realized something. He and Chris were not 'normal' people. They are stars because they are anything but 'normal'. He looked over at Chris and understood that he couldn't contain him and foremost, he shouldn't. If they were going to be a hit and popular, they would need to be their true selves. "Chris."

"Yes Adam." Chris's face was covered in sweat. He constantly had to wipe his brows before the beads of sweat would drop into his eyes.

"Remember what I said about acting all normal and shit?"

"Yeah, I'm loving it." Chris was turning purple.

"Fuck that, do whatever you fucking want." Adam began removing his tie before he even finished his sentence. Chris took in a deep breath and smiled at Adam. They both then looked straight at the elevator door. It opened up on their floor. Chris stepped aside, letting Adam step out first. Adam began walking to his cubicle, Chris following behind him. When they reached it, they stopped. "Sue, if you're at your desk I suggest you step out."

Susan stood up, walked out of her cube and approached Adam, "Hey man, what's going on?"

"I hate my cubicle." Adam then gave a straight kick to the cubicle divider, knocking into his little space, and onto his desk. He kept kicking it until he could hear the computer monitor pop and his desk begin to collapse. People began to get up and out of their cubicles to watch what was going on.

"What the fuck are you doing Adam?" Susan asked.

But, before Adam could answer, Chris interrupted, "You ever fuck a star?" He asked and then slapped her on the ass. Susan punched Chris right on the nose, dropping him to his knees. "Fuck." Was all he said.

Adam looked over and laughed, "Listen Sue, we're done with this whole coming into work nonsense. We don't need it and it's absolutely pointless. You're a cool chick. You're our friend. If you want to join us, feel free to tag along."

"What the hell are you two morons going to do?"

"I don't know." Said Adam.

"Whatever the fuck we want." Answered Chris as he avoided making any eye contact with Susan. She looked down at Chris and then over to Adam. Adam simply shrugged his shoulders and shook his head.

"You two are completely insane. I can't take the same risks that you two can. I don't get to have the same luxuries you guys have, but I do appreciate the offer." She began to walk back into her cubicle.

"Sue wait." Adam called to her.

"What's up?" She asked.

Adam grabbed her by the hand and pulled her closer to him. He then kissed her in a very Hollywood-like manner. A symphony should have been playing in the background as the camera panned out into infinity. "We'll see you around." Said Adam as he helped Chris up from the ground.

Joe A. Melendez

"You sure you don't want to come Sue?" Chris said in a nasally voice as he pinched on the bridge of his nose with his hand.

"Yeah, I'm sure. You boys have fun and don't forget to come visit me." This time Adam didn't call out for her as she walked back into her cubicle.

"You ready to go?" Chris asked Adam.

"Let's do this." They walked out towards the elevators, but before they approached the elevator doors, Chris turned around.

"You all can suck my dick!" He yelled as he grabbed a trashcan that was near by and stepped up onto it. He raised his lit lighter to the fire sprinkler. "I hope you broads wore a good bra today, because your pretty white shirts are about to get soaked." The sprinklers turned on, spraying the entire office space. "Dude, we're taking the stairs this time."

They turned and ran towards the stairwell.

Gotta Get Away

Adam and Chris walked down the stairs slowly. Many of their ex-coworkers, who couldn't stand getting soaked by the sprinklers as they waited for the elevator to come, also took the stairs. As they ran down and passed the two guys, they would curse at them and give them the finger. Adam smiled at them and Chris would just wave. The two where a little wet as well, but neither of them cared. Chris pulled every fire alarm that he passed as they continued down the stairwell. The elevators were now packed with loads of people evacuating the building. People in New York City don't ignore many fire alarms anymore since, you know.

The two finally made it down to the lobby. It was flooded with hordes of people, half of them happy to be distracted from work, the other half pissed to be disturbed. Outside of the building, the flashing lights of fire engines and police vehicles could be seen. Adam and Chris decided to go out the fire exit, since this was technically a fire, sort of. Chris opened it up a bit and caught a glimpse of some cops that saw them; he quickly shut the door shut.

"Dude, I know we could probably get away with some shit, but I don't know if I want to see how much of it we can actually get away with. We need to get out of here." Chris said as he grabbed Adam by the arm and made his way through the crowd towards the other fire exit. They pushed their way through, but stopped when they noticed a shit load of cops pushing their way through the crowd towards them. Adam and Chris were stuck. They didn't know of any other way out.

Then a big large hand reached out from nowhere and grabbed Chris by the arm. Chris was startled and began to yank his arm away until he looked up and recognized the face attached to the meaty arm. It was Hank, the dude from receiving. Hank is an odd fellow and I'll tell you more about him later. "Chris, Adam follow me." He waved for them to come in his direction. The stayed low as they followed Hank towards a large door in the back.

Hank opened the door with a key that he had attached to his belt by a short bungee cord. Once the three were through the door, Hank locked it behind them. "Follow me." He said again, waving his arm again for Adam and Chris to follow. The guys did once again. They walked through a couple of dark and grimy hallways before they made it to another set of doors. Hank stopped here to talk to them.

"Hey first of all, I love you guys."

"Dude, just because you got us away from the cops, doesn't mean we're gonna' get all gay with you now." Chris interrupted Hank.

"Fuck you, don't flatter yourself skinny. I love your show. I watch it every night."

"We're on every night?" Asked Adam.

"You guys are on for a half hour every night, an entire hour on Sunday. Everyone all over the world is watching you guys. If you weren't so big then how do you think they could afford to block off such a large area in Manhattan. You guys have a lot of fans out there, there are only two places that you'll really be able to be safe, one is here and the other is where I'll take you two if you both come with me."

"Dude, we have everything we want here. The cameras don't affect us because we don't even know were they are. They got us hot broads and money. We can do anything that we want. Why should we go with you?" Adam said as he looked over his shoulders.

"Well, like I said, there are two places that you two can truly be safe; but only one where you can really be free and if you think you two are going to get some sweet ass in here… Like I said, you two have a lot of fans and most are not in here. I offer you two freedom, titties and beer."

Chris and Adam looked at each other and without discussing it they both turned to Hank and answered, "Okay."

"Sweet, this door leads to a back alley; I have a van parked out there that we can take out of here. Come on just follow me." Hank opened the doors and checked to make sure that the coast was clear. When he saw that it was, he stepped out and signaled for Adam and Chris to follow. His van was parked out to the left. It was a big blue Club Wagon. Hank slid the side door open for the two guys to get in. When Adam and Chris looked inside there were two gorgeous women sitting down in the van, each was on a different row of seats. Chris and Adam gawked. "I got dibs on the brunette." Said Adam.

"Which one, they're both brunettes."

"The one I'm gonna sit next to." Adam sat next to the one sitting in the second row. Chris sat next to the one in the front row. Hank got into the driver's seat.

"Chris, Adam, I'd like you to meet Amber and Judy," Hank pointed to each one with his open hand as he introduced them, "They live where I'm taking you guys to." He turned around, started the van and drove out of the alleyway.

Adam was talking to Amber, she was the brunette that was sitting next to him and Chris was speaking to Judy, the brunette sitting next to him. Chris excused himself from his conversation with Judy and stood up hunched over and grabbed Adam to sit with him on the back seat. He glanced over to the girls and smiled and then began to speak to Adam.

"What do you think? You think this is really what it seems like or is it another planned adventure?" Chris asked Adam.

"I think it's time we stop caring about that. We seem to have a pretty good thing going for us right here. I'm sure something will fuck it up eventually for us. My guess is that it'll be you somehow."

"Yeah, you're probably right about that. I'll probably take something way too far and just fuck all this right up. So, since that's inevitable I'm gonna go back up to talk some more with that Judy chick. I can't believe we have groupies. We haven't even done anything." Chris got up and sat back next to Judy. Adam got up and returned to sit next to Amber.

"Hey Hank, where we going?" Chris asked.

"We have a nice little thing going for us on some property out in P-A. Don't worry, you two just chill out and relax. You guys are going to have a blast."

Chris turned to Judy and said, "Sounds good to me, how about you?"

"Well, this is probably the most exciting thing that's ever happened to me. You're only the second celebrity I've ever met."

"Oh yeah, so what was the most exciting thing to ever happen to you before this?" Chris asked.

"I guess it would have to be the time that me and my family went down to Universal Studios on the day that they were filming the grand prize give-away for "America's Funniest Videos" and I got to be in the audience."

Chris couldn't blink and when he finally was able to he said, "You're so fucking hot."

"Wow that's funny, that's what the producer said when he picked me to be in the audience and then that's what Bob Saget said before he asked me if I wanted to see his dressing room. He was the first celebrity I ever met"

"Well did you? You know, check out Bob Saget's dressing room?"

"I was going to, but then for some reason when he asked me my age and I told him I was fourteen, he changed his mind."

"Oh that Bob Saget, he sure has good taste."

"What do you mean?"

"Wow. You really are hot. Hey Hank can we stop somewhere for food?"

"Yeah sure, I need to stop for gas anyway. If you guys don't mind just grabbing some corn nuts and beef jerky to hold you over until we reach the ranch."

"Yeah that's cool man." Said Adam.

They arrived shortly at the gas station. Chris, Adam and the girl's hopped out of the Van. Hank went over to pay for the gas.

"Yo Chris, I'm gonna go take a piss. Grab me some shit from inside, grab beer too if they have any." Adam walked towards the side of the building. He headed to the blue door under a restroom sign. Conveniently enough there was another sign on the door saying that it was "Out of Order". "Fuck." Said Adam. He headed to the back of the building. He figured he'd just go to take a piss out back. As he pissed into the trees, he heard some weird noises and voices coming from the woods.

"Yo Adam, hurry the fuck up!" Chris had come around to see what was taking Adam so long, he was holding a plastic bag full of snacks in his hand and two six packs under his arms.

"Hold up, I want to go check something out real quick."

"All right, hold on and wait for me. Let me just put these things down." Chris turned around and handed the things he had in his hands over to Judy and Amber. "We'll be right back." He told them as he turned back around to head towards Adam.

"Hurry up Chris!" Adam yelled.

"Dude, chill out. I'm right here." Chris was standing next to Adam, looking into the woods. "What's up? What do you hear?"

"I'm not too sure but it kind of sounds like some sick religious voodoo rituals are going on down there. I say we go take a look."

"No way man, I've seen this movie before. We'll go in there and find like some kids playing, so we'll head back to the van where we'll find everyone dead with their throats sliced open. Then we'll go inside the gas station to use their phone and then the killer comes out. He kills me first, of course. Then you run out into the woods, where he and his family will eat you."

"Yeah, so what? We'll never know unless we go check it out. Come on." Adam started heading down a small embankment and Chris followed. They both followed the direction of the noises until they both could see something moving in an open field within the woods. "Chris you see that shit?"

"Yeah, what the fuck is that?"

"Seems like some medieval renaissance fair or something. Check that guy out."

Off in the distance, in the middle of the open field was a white-bearded man dressed like a wizard, reciting something from the mind of Tolkien to a bunch of dorks in homemade armor, carrying wooden swords and axes. The old guy was barely audible but he could be heard saying.

"Young warriors, we have waited many moon years for this day to come. The time for our battle with the Orcs of Ramapo is at hand. In the past we have had to postpone this epic battle because of harsh reactions from the elemental gods and a lack of proper transportation last month. But, now we are all here and stronger than ever. With our new level forty-two spell of defense, there is no way that the Orcs can stand a chance against the Mighty Warrior Wizards of Watchung. Today we will celebrate a complete victory for our people!"

He raised his arms up in the air and all his listeners began to chant something that neither Adam nor Chris could make out.

"Yo Adam, check this out." Chris picked up a small rock and moved up closer to the crowd. He managed not to be seen by hiding behind some thick bushes, also the home made helmets these guys were wearing didn't allow them to have the best peripheral vision on earth. Now Chris could hear that the "warriors" were chanting "Watchung!" Chris waited for the right moment and as soon as he saw the bearded man raise his arms once again, he knew it was the perfect time. He beamed the old man right in the breadbasket with the rock. He dropped like a sack of potatoes.

The "warriors" all crowded over the man. They all had looks of fear and shock in their eyes. Chris was laughing too loudly not to be heard. He didn't care. He turned around to look at Adam. "Yo Adam, you see these geeks?" Then he turned back around to see thirty dudes with shitty armor and wooden swords running right towards him. "Oh shit." Said Chris as he turned around to run back up the small drop. "Adam let's go, now!"

Adam didn't need to be told twice or once for that matter, he was already on top. He gave Chris a hand and helped him climb up; then, they sprinted to the van. "Turn the van on!" Yelled Adam. Luckily for the two guys, the shitty armor being worn by the "Mighty Warriors of Watchung" didn't allow for them to have great mobility. They would have never been able to make it up that small embankment before the guys had sped away in the van.

"What the fuck was that about?!" Asked Hank as he drove and chewed on a huge piece of jerky that was sticking out his mouth.

"Well Hank, our lives keep getting weirder and Chris keeps getting stupider every single day. Turns out that some people just don't like getting pelted with rocks and no matter how cowardly you may be, there is something about warrior armor and outnumbering your enemy that makes any man a bloodthirsty killer. We could have kicked their sorry asses if we had two swords of invisibility with level 55 power charm on it."

"Jesus Christ Adam, that's how you found those people. You could smell out your own kind. We should have just left you there with the rest of the geeks."

"Chris, I didn't see you looking too brave when all those "geeks" over there were running out to kill you."

"Fuck you. You suck. I'd rather talk to Judy than keep talking to your sorry ass." Chris turned around to smile at Judy. She and Amber haven't stopped grinning since the guys entered the van. No matter what the two guys said or did, these broads were happier than a fly on shit just to hear it all first hand.

"You shouldn't have pegged Papa Smurf. That was a bad idea." Said Adam.

"Yeah, whatever. They won't even remember about that shit in an hour."

"Whatever Chris."

"Yeah, whatever Adam."

"Whatever."

"Yeah, whatever."

"Whatever."

"Can you two just shut the fuck up?!" Hank yelled out, spitting jerky all over the dashboard and steering wheel. "Sorry guys didn't mean to yell at you all. It's just that I'm on, you know. I'm under a little stress here. They will be looking for you guys, and probably charging me with kidnapping or some shit. So help me, help you and just shut the fuck up for a while."

"Yeah man, come to mention it, why are you doing this for us?" Asked Adam.

"I'll explain everything, once we get to the ranch."

It's been a little more than an hour and a half since they started their trip, the whole "warrior" fiasco lasted only about fifteen minutes. They had about another hour before they would reach their destination. Adam and Chris were becoming more acquainted with the beautiful broads that were bestowed upon them by the mighty Hank. Chris and Adam were never previously familiar with or had experienced what it meant to have groupies. They could have asked for blow jobs or a lesbian show and these two fine young ladies were more than willing to oblige by their orders. Prior to this whole show happening to Adam and Chris, one of the two guys probably would have made such a bold attempt for a cheap thrill; now, they could care less.

Shortly before Chris had the bright idea to feel up Judy's boob, they had arrived to the ranch. They arrived at a wooden gate with the word "Welcome" engraved into a wooden plaque, hanging from an above arch. It all looked pretty much like a regular farm, lots of grass, lots of critters and lots of shit. They had tractors and other equipment scattered around the land. In the center was a rather large building, well it was less like a building and more like a giant house, a really, really big fucking house.

"Welcome home boys, getting ready to enjoy yourselves some real freedom." Hank said with his arms in the air to demonstrate the vastness of the land that surrounded them and the big fucking house in front. "You girls grab unto Adam's and Chris's arm and follow me to the front door. "You guys are about to meet the man responsible for saving your lives and all of ours, for that matter." Hank led the way towards the door. He knocked softly with his knuckles; the door was swiftly opened by two regular looking guys, holding a doorknob in one hand and a can of beer in the other.

"Adam and Chris, welcome to the happiest place on earth. You might not find any Mickey Mouse or Goofy in here, but you sure as hell will find a whole lot of quality booze and pussy. Now follow me inside and let me introduce you to the man that started this whole fucking thing." The group walked into the house and Adam and Chris were overtaken by the furniture and artwork. Someone once said that, "a picture is worth a thousand words"; well, a single picture in this corridor would require at least forty-five thousand words. So do me a favor and try to imagine the house from the "Adams Family", but much cleaner. That's what this place looked like, in color too.

They continued to follow Hank. Adam and Chris were still unsure to whether or not this whole thing was another one of Nadaju's schemes to boost up ratings; neither knew which reality would actually be more comforting to them. So, they just went with it. Hank brought them into a den area adorned with thousands of books, dark mahogany shelves and a large desk in the corner. Behind the desk was a large leather chair with its back towards the guys, a large puff of smoke could be seen coming from the other side.

"Adam Stockton and Chris Gomez, I'd like you to meet the man who has made all this possible, Mr. Johnny Redbone." At that instance, the leather chair rotated around, exposing a ruggedly handsome man wearing a black buttoned down shirt with a red tie. I had a small cigar in my mouth. I pulled the cigar out of his mouth, exposing a smile given to me but a fine orthodontist when I was a kid.

"Hello and welcome to my ranch. My name is Johnny Redbone and I sure am really happy to see you two here. I see that you've met Judy and Amber, such fine pieces of ass, if I could say so myself. You boys should really enjoy them as much as possible; god knows how long it will be 'till their looks vanish." Adam and Chris looked at the girls and received very promising grins from the two. I continued to speak.

"Hank, thank you for bringing the guys here. It will be my pleasure to give you two gentlemen the tour myself. As you can see, this is a very interesting looking place on the inside. I like to keep a low profile from the exterior, if you know what I mean. You can never be too careful about who is watching. But, I'm just preaching to the choir, ain't I guys?" I took another large puff from my cigar, "Sorry guys, how rude of me. Would any of you two like a cigar or a drink?

These are special homegrown cigars from one of our large hydroponics gardens in the complex. It's what pays the bills around here, but I'll explain more to you two as I give you the tour."

"Yeah I'll take one of those." Said Adam.

"Me too and I'll take a drink too." Chris eagerly added.

"Haha, yeah that's the ticket. You guys are here to enjoy yourselves, so if any of you two ever need anything, you let me or Hank know and we'll see what we can do for you."

Johnny Redbone

How you doing? My name is Johnny Redbone, and I've been telling you the story about Adam Stockton and Chris Gomez. We have finally come to the point in the story where I emerge as a character. I'm adding this small section simply as a sort of disclaimer. I have two choices right now. I can be vain and tell you about my many great attributes or I could be humble about my autobiographical description. Neither of these choices would be fair to you nor me. So I'll try to be as objective as possible.

I grew up on the streets of New Jersey, right across the Hudson River parallel to Manhattan. I had to learn about life on my own, from a very mean and crude source. Luckily I was born with many gifts, a good mind, a healthy body, and a pretty face. I was poor and on the streets and needed to use these gifts to get me the fuck out of there. I hustled and conned my way out of that shitty place and eventually came to be in charge of that beautiful and wonderful "crop"-farm that Adam and Chris were taken to.

I'll spare you any more details because this is not my story to be told, but that of Adam and Chris. So for now, I'll continue with the story.

Just Keep Reading

I lifted a small wooden humidor from off my desk and offered Adam and Chris a cigar from inside of it. They both took one and before either of them could even place them in their mouths, Amber and Judy had lit wooden matches hovering in front of their faces. Judy also had a beer for Chris in her free hand.

"Okay gentlemen, now that we have all the tools of the trade that we need, let me take you on the grand tour of the place." I walked past them and stood at the door, holding it steadily for Adam and Chris to walk through. As they walked down the corridors, I would explain some of the art that adorned the walls. I told them how some were purchased and others were actually created by some of the house residents. It all began to get a lot more interesting for the two, once the contents of the cigars started to take a hold of them.

"Dude, this is some kick ass weed. You grow this shit here?" Chris asked with chinky eyes and a retarded smile, it was the same face that he would put on when taking a massive shit.

"Yes Chris, don't worry. I'll show you the gardens later. First I'd like you to meet your new roommates. It's dinner time right now, so everyone should be in the dining area." We arrived to a set of giant wooden doors. I knocked softly on them and shortly after the doors were being opened from the inside. "Here we are at the dining room." The dining room was enormous; it was about the size of a high school gym, with a ceiling almost as high. There were a bunch of tables, much like a banquet hall. Collectively, sitting at the tables, there were around thirty people. I'd count for you, but I'm too lazy. "Adam and Chris, I'd like you to meet your new roommates."

Chris and Adam walked in and waved hello. Adam said, "Hey, how you guys doing?" Chris simply continued to smoke his cigar and drink his beer. The people sitting down were now all standing up and mumbling things amongst themselves. But right before Adam and Chris really began to feel awkward, a rather large, bearded, longhaired man came rushing towards them with a big smile.

"Welcome guys!" He bellowed out as he picked up Adam and bear-hugged him. "We're so happy you two are here and we're all very glad that you can be part of our family now." He put down Adam, gave a friendly smack on the face to Chris and laughed. Chris took another sip of his beer and a pull from his cigar. "They call me Big D. We'll have some drinks later." Big D went back to his table and as he did, the others stood up and walked over to greet the two.

It was an interesting looking crowd. Some of the people, both men and women, were heavily tattooed and pierced, others were long-haired and in hippy garb, while yet others looked like regular people. The one thing that definitely stood out, in both Adam's and Chris's eyes, was the abundance of hot women. Some of the more friendly women gave Chris and Adam a kiss on the lips and yet, the most friendly ones felt free to grab a hold of Adam and Chris's packages as they said hello.

I simply stood back, smoking my cigar and smiling as the two met all of the people. Once everyone had introduced themselves to them, I spoke, "Ladies and Gentlemen, joining our family are these two, 'Just Ruthless' men, Adam Stockton and Chris Gomez. I think we can all learn a lot from these two men in the ways of honesty and a kick-ass outlook on life. We will treat them, as we would want them to treat us and we will accommodate any desires that they need to be fulfilled. Now I want you all to finish your dinner in peace, while I continue to give these two fine men the tour of our complex."

I led the way. As we walked out of the room, the crowd began to holler and cheer in a very rowdy and heartfelt way. The guys looked back and waved to them just before the doors were closed.

"We know about what they did to you guys," I told them. "They lied to you so that they could make a profit; but you guys are great. You two not only know how to have a good time, but you've handled yourselves so exceptionally during the charades they put you two through. This is why we invited you guys to stay here. We're just a bunch of fun-loving people, trying to do our thing and not bother anybody. We have a good time."

"So, do they air us live or do they edit the shit first?" Asked Adam.

"Um... I think they edit the show a bit." I replied

"You wouldn't happen to have any of the shows recorded, would you?"

"Yeah man, we have TiVo. I tell you what we're going to do. We're going to have a little party to celebrate your arrival. We're gonna have all sorts of good booze, good smokes, some other goodies, you've already seen the caliber of broads that we have in here, and we've even got a band to play. It's gonna be a fun time. I'm sure we'll all be up late night, so maybe we'll watch the show then. If not, there's time. Then you guys will get to experience your lives through the eyes of someone else."

"Sounds good to me." Said Adam.

"Yeah man, everything so far has been pretty sweet. It sounds good to me, too." Added Chris.

"Good, I'm glad to hear that. You know? I bet you two are a bit tired. I'll show you to your room. Yes, I said room. You two will be sharing a room. As you can tell, we have a lot of people living here and the rooms are not as common as we wished they could be, so most of us have to share. Just follow me this way. This room is yours." I opened the door. "As you can see, it's a pretty large room you guys have to share. We stocked the drawers and the closets with clothes we got for you guys, some of them are new, most of them are second hand.

On the desk to the back, you can find a carton of smokes, two bottles of good bourbon and some other things you two might enjoy. I'm sure you guys are probably hungry so I'll send up some food for you two in a bit. You guys eat, sleep and be merry and we'll come get you when its time to party. We start our parties late, so you guys don't worry, you'll have plenty of time to relax and soak it all in. See you both later and once again, I'm very happy that you two could join us."

"Yeah, no problem. See you later." Adam said to me as he walked into the room and shut the door. Chris had been already fucking around with shit that was in, on, or around the general vicinity of the desk.

"Dude, check out all this shit. They gave us booze, cigarettes, condoms, an ounce each of some crazy smelling weed and check this out." Chris lifted up a sandwich zip-lock bag full of golden caps and stems of the most disgusting look mushrooms ever created. Chris opened it up and a cloud of rank smell filled the room immediately.

"Oh man, that's fucking disgusting. Close the fucking bag. I hope they left us candles or something somewhere on that damn desk too." Adam began to go through the drawers of the desk.

"Wow, this shit wreaks. I'm so gonna eat some tonight. Are you in?" Chris held the bag in front of Adam's face.

With a look of disgust on his face Adam replied, "Fuck no, shrooms fuck up my stomach. But ask me later when I can't make good judgments anymore." Adam found some incense and a lighter in one of the desk's drawers. He lit it and almost immediately the funk of the shrooms began to disappear.

"Alright man, suit yourself. I'm still gonna e…" Before Chris could finish what he was saying, there was a knocking on the door. Chris dropped the bag on the desk and went to open the door. Still accustomed to living in an apartment building where religious maniacs with machetes were known to roam the hallways at night, Chris asked, "Who's there?" before he opened the door.

"It's us, Amber and Judy. We've brought you guys some food." Chris didn't hesitate to open the door after that answer.

"Holy tits, come right in." Chris, so gallantly said as he let the two ladies into the room.

"Welcome ladies. Before you two say anything, there is something that I'd like to say real quickly. The bed by the window is mine. I called dibs." Adam had been having his eye on that bed ever since I opened the door.

"Dude, that's fucking fine. That just means that I have more wall to put my shit up on." Chris said with a smile.

"What are you in fucking high school?" Adam asked Chris.

"Look who's talking, the asshole that is more concerned about what bed he stakes rather than eating these two fine dishes that just walked in though our door." Chris looked over and smiled to Judy and Amber after he made his very triumphant point to Adam.

Adam had a dumbfounded look on his face as he looked over at Amber and asked, "Hey Amber, what's going on? What you got there?" Adam walked over to her and grabbed the plate from her hands. He sat on his bed right next to the window. "Why don't you have a seat right here next to me on my bed. This one right here, next to the window." Adam smiled and patted the space next to him.

"I hope you get sick sleeping next to that thing," said Chris. "I meant the window, not you Amber." Chris walked over to Judy and grabbed the plate of food in one hand and grabbed Judy with the other. He sat on his bed, the one with all the wall behind it, and brought down Judy with him. "I'll tell you what. Judy do me a favor and hold my plate again. I'm going to have a quick sit at this desk and roll us a nice fat joint with this wonderful smelling bud that our hosts have so kindly bestowed upon us. Then we're going to smoke it and hang out...."

As Chris rambled on, Adam ate his food without lifting his eyes from the plate. He began to think about this situation that he was in. He knew that it was too good to be true, or at least he felt it to be. The pleasure that Adam got from making people uncomfortable was a way for him to distract himself from his monotonous life. Lately, there has been nothing monotonous or mundane about his daily routine; in actuality, there has been no routine in Adam's life for the past several months. As he finished his plate of food, he finally came back to reality and the conversation that Amber and Judy were having.

"This is a really fun place to live. Johnny really is an awesome guy."

"You guys are really lucky to be here."

It doesn't matter which one of the girls said what, but Adam began to get a little agitated. "You girls have to go."

"Why, I thought we were going to…. Well, you know. Johnny wanted us to make you feel comfortable." Amber said with a puzzled look on her face.

"It's been a long day and we'll catch up later, but right now I need to get some rest. So, I need to ask you two girls to leave." Adam handed Amber his plate and pointed to the door. The two girls stood up and walked out of the room, Adam closed the door behind them.

"Adam, someone is at the door." Chris, totally oblivious to what just happened, said as he licked closed the joint he had rolled.

"No dude, I asked Judy and Amber to leave."

"What are you fucking kidding me?" Chris quickly turned around and looked around the room. "When did this happen?"

"Just now, you must have heard the entire thing."

"Nope, I zone out when I'm hard at work."

"I'm sure that's why you were such an expert mail-guy."

"Go fuck yourself Adam. No really, go for it. Apparently, you prefer to fuck yourself, because you just kicked out two smoking hot broads that were sent here, to this room, for no other reason than to pleasure us. Now, because of that, I'm going to smoke this joint by myself." Chris leaned back on the chair and lit the joint. He puffed on it a couple of times before he extended his arm towards Adam, handing him the joint.

"I thought you were going to smoke it by yourself?" asked Adam.

"Shut up and smoke it." Adam took the joint from Chris's hand. Chris continued to speak while Adam hit it. "I know what's bothering you. You don't really want any of this. You can't stand the spotlight. I love all this. The women, the money, the adventure, the fame, all this is what I always wanted, but I got your back. Whatever you want to do, I'm in.

You want Susan, don't you?"

Adam handed the joint back to Chris and rolled over on his side, his back towards Chris. "I'm taking a nap. We'll talk later."

Heaven on Earth

Chris and Adam were both snoring when there came a knocking at the door. Chris had fallen asleep on the desk chair. Somehow he remained perfectly balanced on the hind legs of the chair with his feet up on the desk. The two didn't even hear the knocking the first time. The second time, the knocking came a little harder. This startled Chris enough to make him lose his balance and fall backwards unto the floor.

"I'm fucking coming!" Yelled Chris. Adam was hiding his head under a pillow, trying to muffle out the sounds. "Fucking cocksucker." Chris was rubbing the back of his head with his hand; he had hit it pretty hard on the way down, luckily for him, his head is made of steel. He opened the door and there stood Big D.

"Hey, Hey! What is Up?!" Big D said very excitedly as he picked up Chris in a bear hug.

Chris mumbled something.

"What did ya, say?" Asked Big D. "I can't hear ya."

Chris's face began to turn beet red, his eyes were opening wider and he began to foam at the mouth. His breath was being forced right out of him. Then came a thundering head-but from Chris that caught Big D directly between the eyes. Big D quickly dropped Chris onto the ground and stumbled backwards until his back met the wall, then his knees buckled and he slid down until his ass finally hit the ground. He had a blank look on his face. At this point, Adam had already been watching Big D bear hugging Chris and got up as soon as he saw the head but. He walked over to the door.

Adam looked down at Big D. Big D was staring straight into space. Meanwhile, Chris was still gasping for air on the ground between Adam's legs. Adam began to laugh and walked back into the room. He grabbed a glass of water that had been resting on the desk. He turned around and walked back towards Big D. On his way, he managed to kick Chris out of the way. A quick boot to the ribs did the job just fine. He stopped at the door and threw the contents of the glass on to Big D's face. Big D looked up at Adam with his eyes drooping and shook his head.

"What the fuck happened?" Asked Big D.

"You two boys got carried away. It started with some heavy petting but then it just got all out of hand. Seriously guys, next time just shake hands. Let me help you up." Adam stretched out his hand and tried his hardest to help pick up Big D, but Big D isn't called Big D because he has a twelve-inch penis, which he does.

Why else do you think that he's always so happy?

By this point, Chris had managed to get back up on his feet. He walked over to the desk to take a sip from his water, but it wasn't there. So, he grabbed one of the bottles of whiskey, cracked it open and took a healthy swig. He quickly began to regret that action. You could tell by the face that he had on, it was similar to the one that he had right before he head butted Big D. I guess you can call it the "fight or fucked" look. Adam still struggled with Big D.

"Yo asshole. How about you give me a hand?" Adam asked Chris as he managed to get Big D's arm around his neck. Chris was finally able to begin to speak and breathe normally at this point.

"Holy Jesus fuck. That guy is a beast. My head is fucking killing me." Chris walked over and put Big D's other arm around his neck. Adam and Chris were able to lift him between the two and walk him over to Adam's bed, where Big D was able to sit down.

"Damn Chris, you have a fucking hard head." Big D said as he rubbed his forehead, trying to ease the pain.

"Some people say it's made of steel. Rumor has it that he lost the front piece of his skull in a head banging accident. A huge black man was banging his mom while she was pregnant with him, and Chris's dome happened to absorb quite a bit of the blow." Adam smiled as he grabbed the bottle of booze from Chris's hand. He handed it over to Big D. "Have some of this. It'll make it better now and you'll feel extra shitty tomorrow, but that's the American way."

"Thanks Adam." Big D took a healthy chug. "I actually came up here to tell you guys that the party starts in a half hour."

At that moment, I appeared at the door. "Hello boys, thought you'd guys be downstairs by now." I continued walking in towards Big D. I grabbed the bottle out of his hand, took a sip and passed it over to Chris. "I see you got a little sidetracked D. What the fuck?"

"Sorry Johnny, we got a little carried away in here. These guys are all right." Big D said as he was finally able to stand up.

"Of course they are. If they weren't, they'd probably be trying to get themselves out of some other wacky adventure." I said as he looked over at Adam and then Chris. I needed to assert my alpha male position, if nothing more than for personal amusement. I had no problem with any of those dudes in that room.

"Who says we're not?" Adam smiled as he waited for my reaction.

He wasn't going to outwit me in my own house. "I ask you Adam to ask yourself that same question later. If you do, you're free to leave and come back anytime you want. But before you get too paranoid, let me tell you. You boys are going to have a hell of a time tonight. So how about you two get dressed and come join us downstairs? Big D, you wait for these guys outside their room and escort them down when they're ready and Big D, no fucking around this time. I'll see you all in a bit."

I walked out and went on my way. I had certain things to take care of. "I better do what he says." Big D said as he walked out behind me. He didn't say that out of fear, Big D could have crushed me if he wanted to, but I'd earned my respect from everyone in that place.

Adam and Chris did what they had to do to make themselves pretty, but in actuality the best thing that they have in their favor to make them better looking is the lack of lighting and overabundance of drugs and alcohol that awaited for them downstairs. "Hey Adam, how do I look?" There was no mirror in their room, so Adam tried his best to give Chris his expert opinion on fashion.

"You look fine, except for around the face region. Come here so I can pound some good looks into you with this bottle." Adam had picked up the bottle of bourbon and began to walk towards Chris.

"You come any closer and I swear on your mother that I'm gonna fuck you up." Chris stood in a defensive posture. Adam had completed his job, to distract Chris enough for him to forget to zipper his pants up.

"Sorry Chris, sometimes I get carried away, but you hang loose. Don't be afraid to put yourself out there tonight and show everyone what you've got. You must show them you've got balls and that you're not afraid to put them out there for the world to see. So come on let's go." Adam walked out of the room and Chris followed. Chris made sure to close his pant's zipper before he stepped out.

"Adam, you're an asshole." Chris said as he joined the guys in the hallway.

Big D led the way through the hallway in front of Adam and Chris. They went downstairs back to the dining room area. The place looked a lot different from when the guy's first saw it. During the day, it looked like a VFW banquet hall, set up with multiple round tables, but at night it resembled a classy ballroom. The lights were low and the room was filled with smoke and red lighting. There was a bar to the right with a gorgeous brunette tending it, wearing a tiny devil costume and red horns.

At the back of the room was a stage. It was elevated about 3 feet up off of the ground; a large red curtain covered the stage. People were sitting at the tables, which had black cloths covering them and buckets full of ice with bottles of champagne. The people were all dressed in their best attire, and when speaking about this group, means that it looked like a fucking freak show. Black suits and red dresses, tattoos and hair, wonderful nudity and atrocious exhibitionism, these all blended in together to make a very Victorian depiction of Dante's Inferno only a little weirder and a lot sexier.

Chris turned to me and asked, "This isn't some kind of gay satanic cult, is it?"

"No Chris, there's no religion in this house. We just like to have a good time. Come on in, you guys are sitting with me tonight."

"Just tonight?" Asked Adam.

"Well, after tonight, you can sit wherever the fuck you want." I said as I led the way. We were seated at a table towards the right of the stage, where Amber, Judy and another two girls sat waiting. Adam sat next to Amber, Chris next to Judy and I sat right between the other two girls. Fuck yeah. We had all just sat down and gotten comfortable when I decided to sand up and ask for everyone's attention. Once they all did I began to speak.

"Imagine a life without sex. Sex is the most powerful natural instrument that has ever had any type of control over mankind. It IS the meaning of life. It's the reason why we were put on earth to do all the stupid things that we do. It is also rightfully the reason why we do all the stupid things that we do. At some point in history, there was a lot of fucking going on. People were having all sorts of great sex, anywhere and anytime they wanted with whomever they wanted. There were no rules.

Then some assholes had to fuck it up for the rest of them.

Have you ever wondered why the tree that bore the apple that ruined Adam and Eve's innocence was called "the Tree of Knowledge"? As soon as Adam ate that apple and he took a real good look at Eve's hot, furry-Australopithecus Africanus-gorilla tits, he jumped all over that beet red baboon ass. Then a lot of fucking occurred. We fucked the fur off our bodies. We fucked different types of skin color and bone structures to create wonderful groups of unique humans. Those humans fucked like crazy for tens of thousands of years and things were going just fine. But then things changed.

We evolved mentally. We became the smartest creatures on earth and were able to have a greater survival rate. According to Darwin's idea of natural selection, the strongest and smartest survive. However, with this same highly evolved intelligence that allowed the fittest man and woman to prosper, a high sense of emotion was also acquired. We began to care for our own kind. It was a noble time until the stupid began to survive. The intelligent protected the stupid from disease and danger. They created things to make all their lives easier and everything went well for a while.

Then some intelligent people began to realize that there were a lot of stupid people on the planet and that the stupid people were easily controlled by being told make believe tales. Stories created to scare and control were so brilliantly hidden amongst a humble philosophy. It took both self-responsibility and the fun and enjoyment of sex away from everyone. Those who don't like to think rather be told what to do. These people who made up these stories were scumbags, but those who believe them are worse.

The reason that I tell you this is because we live in a country being run by some very sexually repressed scumbags. They have never had a good old fashion fucking. I don't give a shit what gets you off, if it's girls, boys, or both. If you like using toys, or role-playing or exhibitionism, that's cool. There needs to be a place for those of us who feel able enough to make our own decisions and I like to think that this is that kind of place.

Our friends, Chris Gomez and Adam Stockton join us here today. We want them to feel at home, they should have a good time and don't allow them to become sexually repressed assholes.

Tonight, we're going to party."

With that said, I popped open a bottle of champagne and was joined in doing so by the other members at the other tables as they also all popped their bottles, spraying champagne all over the crowd and room.

Before the champagne stopped flowing, the band began to play on stage.

The band was playing and the booze was flowing. Drug use was very openly displayed. Each table had a small glass mirror and a fresh razor blade, things that a more humble man might confuse for other things that are required for a pre-dinner, pre-show, shaving ritual.

Now bear with me, because this night was a bit blurry. I remember that the name of the band was "The Longnecks"; it's the name I saw drawn on to the bass drum. Animal from the Muppets was playing the drums.

I simply call it, how I recall it.

The lead singer, bassist and guitarist all wore Mexican, lucha-libre masks. The lead singer had a blue-metallic mask and wore no shirt, exposing his very macho, hairy chest. The bassist was a large man with a white mask with silver designs around the sides. He wore a white leotard, much like the black one that Andre the giant used to wear. The bassist wore a cat-like mask with whiskers and fur. He wore a full leotard cat suit with orange and black tiger stripes.

Later on, Adam and Chris would find out that their names are Huevos Azul, Santo Blanco, and The Great Catino and that they always wear the masks, at all times. Although, some suspect that they take them off at night to sleep; however, no pictures or proof exists. And Animal, is actually Animal from the Muppets, I'm not lying to you. By the way, Animal doesn't get high, if you were wondering. He's all about the kids. He used to jam with Gary Glitter back in the day.

The Longnecks played songs of sex, violence and lucha-libre. They chugged on bottles of Jim Beam and spat at the crowd. The audience was going insane. It wasn't that much after the band started playing that the amount of drugs and alcohol being consumed began to take a hold of those partaking. Everyone had been pre-gaming awaiting the arrival of Adam and Chris.

Tits and cock grabbing filled the front of the stage. Big D jumped up on stage, dropped his pants and exposed the tattoo on his ass, which read, "Rock Roll". I'm assuming that there was an "N" somewhere around where his giant furry ass crack scares little children from. I'll save you all the disgust by being less descriptive. Big D would do this every time there was a show and by now most of the people have gotten used to the sight of it all.

Adam and Chris laughed.

Eventually, the drugs and alcohol caught up with Adam and Chris, too. Chris took his shirt off and grabbed Judy; he pulled her towards the stage. They began jumping around and dancing. Judy took her shirt off, too. Nobody cared. I sat in the empty chair next to Adam.

"Having fun!?" I asked Adam, having to yell a bit in order to be heard over the music.

"I'm having a blast!" Adam replied.

I got a lot closer to Adam's ear.

"You don't look like you're having too much fun. There are plenty of girls here, drugs, alcohol…. Shit, even the band is kick ass. So what the fuck? You're not having fun?"

Adam got closer to my ear.

"I don't trust you. All this seems to me like another plot from the TV guys. I have to admit that, so far, this one has been the most enjoyable. But, I can't trust it all. It's too good to be true." Adam backed unto his chair.

"Come with me!" I yelled to Adam, as I stood and called him over with my hand.

Adam followed me out of the ballroom.

As soon as the doors closed, I began to speak.

"First of all, let me show you something that will help me explain all this to you." I started walking down the hallway towards the kitchen. Once in the kitchen I headed to the freezer. It was a giant aluminum freezer with a huge swinging door. I swung it open, revealing a small frozen room. I walked into the freezer and turned left. I pressed on the wall and a small number pad appeared next to my hand. I entered a combination of numbers and the wall slid open.

I motioned for Adam to follow him. Adam did. We went down some steps into a giant underground marijuana nursery. I began to speak again.

"This right here, Adam, is why I brought you guys here. This is how we can afford to have this place, and all the nice things within its walls. Freedom doesn't come without a cost."

We walked past the array of plants, lights and all the other things needed to grow good pot in a giant basement. The next room was full of guns and other weapons.

"You see all these? I don't ever want to have to use these weapons. Using these weapons against the cops would be like using a glass of water to fight a forest fire. We have a very good thing going for us here and I'd hate for all those good people up there to have to lose it all. I don't want to be held responsible for the loss of their lives.

'What does this have to do with you guys?' You're probably asking yourself.

The people who live here are not the only people that work for this cause, the cause being of course, this freedom to live our lives how we chose. So I have a lot of friends all over the place. I've been able to accomplish all this because of two things, one is my uncanny ability to judge good people, and the other is my good luck.

I enjoyed watching your show.

You two seemed authentic so I decided to take a risk. Either you two were full of shit and just acting, in which way you would have both been buried upside down out back, or you two were actually, authentic and honest. In my opinion, those are the two greatest characteristics that any human can have. I like to think that everyone living in this nutty house is at the very least authentic and honest.

I think that in the short time that we have spent with each other, I have been able to make my decision about you two. I've decided that Chris is cool but you have to go."

Adam didn't hesitate to take a swing at me. Fortunately for the two of us, I was quicker. I managed to dodge Adam and grab him before anything could get too out of hand.

"Whoa, I was just kidding. You're cool too. But, I can tell that you don't want to be here. Funny thing is that neither do I. Let me tell you about this plan that I have. "

I told him about my situation and some information that I thought he would find both amusing and useful. Don't worry, you'll find out eventually. You don't get the option of the short version.

"What do you think? It works out for you too. What will you do later, what do you want?" I asked after telling Adam the wonderful plan.

"First of all, that's a mighty good plan. I have a feeling that Chris will be pretty excited about it when he finds out. But to answer your question, I've been thinking a lot lately about my life. I've come to the conclusion that I don't want sex, drugs and rock n roll. All that I want is a little bit of peace, privacy and someone's companionship."

"Who do you want?"

"Well, there's this chick at work. Her name is Susan." Before Adam could finish what he had to say, I had to interrupt him.

"Ha! I fucking knew it! Man, your show rocks!"

"Um, well, thanks… but I don't have much to do. It's actually my life. But, as I was saying.

I think I love Susan. She doesn't annoy me. She's pretty. She's interesting. She really doesn't annoy me, which is a rare trait in people. I think about her all the time, how I wish sometimes that everything was back the way it was without all the craziness. But, you see, I don't want that either. I just want to be able to see Susan again, in peace.

I need to go back to her, that's where my mind and my heart are. Like I said before, I have a feeling that Chris is going to love your plan. We'll tell him later."

"Sounds good. You're a good man Adam Stockton. You might want Susan and only Susan, but I, on the other hand, have a couple of girls that I'd like to give tongue bathes to. Now lets go back upstairs and get fucked up."

I led the way out the weapons room, through the underground gardens, up the stairs, out of the freezer, out the kitchen, down the hall and back into the ballroom. We went back to our table. The band was still playing and Chris and Judy were still dancing.

I sat between his two girls and gave each a pretty disgusting kiss; I then had them kiss each other in the same, but not disgusting at all, way. I looked beyond the kissing girls and gave Adam, who was enjoying the display, a wink.

Adam looked over to Amber and smiled. He got closer to her and whispered something into her ear. She got up and walked towards the stage. She began dancing near Chris and Judy and took off her shirt too. Then she began to make out with Judy. Chris stopped dancing and just stared and smiled. He looked over at Adam, who had been watching, and gave him a thumbs up.

Chris then continued to stare and stare, as Judy and Amber made out topless in front of him on the dance floor. He stared and stared. He continued to stare. Then Chris began to get frustrated. He walked back to the table and sat next to Adam. He leaned over and whispered into Adam's ear.

"You're such an asshole." Chris sat back, took a swig of his drink and lit up a cigarette. I tapped him on the shoulder.

"Dude, no smoking in here!" I yelled at Chris. Before Chris could get angry, I handed him something. "Smoke this instead."

Chris put the joint in his mouth and lit it. He was happy once again.

The band played a while longer, but as the night progressed, the crowd diminished. I disappeared with my two girls, leaving Adam alone to sit at the table. He didn't want to have to talk to any other insane characters that night, so he headed back to his room. Chris and the two girls eventually came back to the table, when they saw no one else was left at the table, they decided to finish the party back at the girls' room. They all slept real well that night and they rightfully deserved it.

What Do you Want?

Chris eventually made it back to the room. Adam had fallen asleep on his own bed with a bottle of champagne grasped in his talons. When Chris entered the room he made as much noise as any drunkard would make when trying to be extra quiet; doors were slammed, chairs were dropped, and gases were emitted. However, Adam didn't wake up until Chris tried to be a good friend and remove the bottle from Adam's hands. Chris had underestimated Adam's grip and when he yanked at the bottle, he slipped and the bottle knocked Adam directly on the forehead.

"Ahhhh! What the fuck?!"

The pain was too intense to allow Adam to open up his eyes. It didn't help that Adam had not yet slept off the hangover that would haunt him for most of the day. Now his head was throbbing in pain, his eyes began to tear and his stomach began to turn. By the time that Adam was able to open his eyes, Chris was sound asleep on his bed. Adam stood up and held on to the desk chair. His balance wouldn't come back to him fully for another twenty minutes. Aside from the pressure in his head, Adam felt an intense pressure in his bladder.

"Where the fuck is the bathroom?" He asked out loud even though he knew that he would not receive an answer. He looked down at Chris, as he slept on his bed, and couldn't help but smile for his friend. Chris was lying, belly down, on his mattress, wearing only his boxers, one shoe and a giant smile. He had crumpled up the rest of his clothes into a ball and was now using it as a pillow.

"Chris. Psss. Chris. Where's the bathroom?" Adam whispered. There was no answer. He thought about messing with him, but the pressure to urinate was beginning to become unbearable. He turned around and left the room. The hallway was dark and cold, Adam had no shoes on and the frigid floor was not helping his problem. He decided to go downstairs; he had used the bathroom near the ballroom the night before, and figured it was his best bet. But, before he made it to the stairs, he noticed a door slightly ajar to his right. He peeked in and saw a sink and a shower.

Those are the kind of things that one normally finds in the bathroom, so Adam walked in. Much to Adam's surprise there was a Mexican wrestler asleep on the toilet, by the look of the furry mask; it must be The Great Catino. Luckily for Adam, the sink was unoccupied. Adam was kind enough to run the water as he pissed into the sink. He heard a farting sound and neither he nor the wrestler on the toilet had done it. He peeked behind the shower curtain and saw another wrestler passed out with a bottle of mescal. It was the monster of a man known as El Santo Blanco. Adam thought nothing of it. He finished his business and left the bathroom.

The floor was bone chilling, so Adam hurried back to the room. Chris had not budged, nor was he expected to budge for a while, much like Adam before until Chris woke him up. Adam thought about messing with Chris, but then decided that too much noise might actually make his own head explode. He lay down on his bed and closed his eyes. He would have loved to have been able to simply fall asleep and pass out and wake up feeling fresh, but the pounding headache and the upset stomach were giving him a hard time. Then, he started to think.

Adam thought about his life. He though about how he wanted so little, but it would cost so much to attain. He had thought that this mess that he naively got himself into would actually bring him that which he most wanted. He was mistaken. He didn't want to milk this opportunity for all that he could. He wanted to be left alone and to once again be able to disappear into the crowd. This ability to stay out of the spotlight was what allowed Adam to be the person that he was.

I was absolutely correct when I told Adam that I believed that he and Chris were authentic and honest. Every person, at some point in their life, is authentic and honest, but people like Adam, Chris, and I like to think that I'm on that list are like this more often. Adam didn't want to share his authenticity with total strangers. To Adam, having a poisonous tongue brought him a sense of pleasure. He enjoyed the cringing and the humiliation that his words have caused people to feel in the past. The things he said were unexpected and out of line with what a normal, dishonest, unauthentic person would say.

The world was changing because of Adam. He didn't quite realize the extent just yet. Adam's crudeness was being copied, much like any other stupid catchphrase that infiltrates our lives through popular culture, now it was trendy and hip to be crass. Adam understood the consequences that his honesty might bring to himself and others. Many people did not.

Adam never felt that he was rude to anyone that didn't deserve it. There might have been times where he felt that he had crossed the line, but he doubted that anyone actually listened to the things he said. Many people disregard honesty as the truth. Adam unknowingly impacted a couple of people, some of who you have never heard of and might never hear about, but one in particular was a heavy-set woman who Adam had come in contact with on the elevator of his old office building. After Adam's comments, she went home and decided to try a new diet and exercise regiment. She has since lost twenty pounds and is now working as Nadaju's assistant.

Adam's honesty was now becoming a worldwide phenomenon. People all over the globe were telling off their bosses, telling their spouses the truth, writing letters to their local politicians, protesting more injustices and protesting the television show "Just Ruthless". You see, with honesty comes a lot of anger. Like I said before, people don't like to hear the truth and ever since it has become so popular, violence and murder has gone up thirty-five percent and several countries are now in the brink of civil wars. Adam and Chris were still unaware of these things, but when they eventually do find out they reply with.

"Dumbasses"

"Fuck them."

I forget who said which.

Adam then thought about how he has been blatantly honest with everyone except Susan. He has cared for her for a long time and has never been able to tell her. Maybe he had never truly realized it until now, but even so, he felt that he should have thought about it sooner.

He sat up and packed a bowl. He smoked it and lay back down. His stomach was feeling better, but his head was still throbbing. He clenched his eyes closed for a while; it made his headache go away momentarily. The kaleidoscope in his skull brought a sense of euphoria to Adam for a while, a brief instance of peace and tranquility. It was quiet and sobering. Adam had past on any more thoughts for the moment. He was pretty content for his inability to process any more of these thoughts that had been plaguing him endlessly for the past couple of days.

He felt as if he should make fun of himself for being stupid enough to wanting to leave all this being handed to him, for one woman. He never really thought about himself beyond the present. He just was. He did what needed to get done to get by, nothing more and nothing less. He had the ability to change the world, as was now being proven, but he never actually thought that he would ever be in a position which would allow him to do so.

Adam liked to fuck with people because he saw the world a little differently. He saw himself as someone who is no better or worse than anyone else, so he never felt the need to tell a lie. When you lie to someone, you do so because that person does not agree with what you actually should tell them, the truth. He knew they wouldn't like the truth so you tell them a lie. He didn't feel that lying was healthy or necessary. It wasted a lot of valuable time and energy that Adam could need some other time to waste at his leisure. So the fact that he had been trying his best in life to avoid being noticed and was now known by almost the entire world, would come as too weird for Adam. It made him very uncomfortable.

He had seen people as very unauthentic before. Now, he couldn't trust anyone, except for Chris and Susan. His decision of Susan over Chris actually came pretty easily to Adam. Chris doesn't have a vagina. Susan does and she has tits, too. She also is prettier and smells a lot better. Chris never had a chance. Adam was at peace. He fell asleep.

Rerun

The next day didn't quite start as early as I had first anticipated. Adam had awoken before Chris did. He had gotten himself together and washed up and met up with Hank and I in my office. We were bullshitting for a while, talking about the plan, how great it is and how wonderful it would turn out.

Chris eventually woke up. He rolled over unto a pool of saliva that had cooled to room temperature. He wouldn't have minded it so much, if it didn't make his bladder swell up two fold. That shot Chris right into consciousness and right up off his bed. He placed a hand up on the wall to help him balance out the negative forces that were making his head throb with agony. With only his boxers on, he stumbled out the bedroom door, once again; he placed his hands up on the wall to help him keep his balance.

Much like Adam had found the bathroom previously, Chris happened to stumble, literally, into the open door. He managed to catch himself on the doorframe, but the door still swung open pretty violently. Inside, there no longer dwelled slumbering masked luchadores; instead, were two gorgeous girls. The black one's name is Sherry Washington and the tall Amazonian's name is Kelu, pronounced KEE – LOO.

Sherry was a hot piece of ass. She was a painter. Sherry was strikingly beautiful. I have seen many beautiful women in my life. Some I have even been lucky enough to see up close. The craziest amongst those have actually let me touch them, and yet some were so completely insane to have slept with me! I think I can safely say that Sherry is fine.

Kelu was huge. She came to us from a far off land where Vikings once ruled. Where they, through physical selection, grabbed the fittest women throughout Europe and bred with them for generations to create giant, big breasted, gorgeous Amazonians like this here Kelu. Kelu was not as striking as Sherry was, but there was something about her that made your dick harder than it has ever been. This effect made Chris dizzier than he already was. He couldn't catch his breath right away, so Kelu and Sherry grabbed him and sat him down on the toilet.

Hank, Adam and I were chatting when Chris stumbled into the room, still only wearing his boxers.

"Four in less than twelve hours. I had sex with four of the hottest broads I have ever met in my life in less than twelve hours. Two at a time, TWICE!" Chris walked over and shook my hand; he then turned to shake Hank's, and then shook Adam's hand. "Thank you Mr. Redbone for having such a kick-ass place, thank you Hank for bringing us here and thank you Adam for getting us here." Chris stood there at the door in nothing more than his boxers, with his fists on his sides and his chin in the air, much like the patriotic superman pose.

"Actually Chris, we were just discussing that," Adam began to speak. "There's something I need to tell you. I'm going to leave this place. I'm heading back home to find Susan."

"Dude, that is great!" Chris replied.

"That's what I'm saying!" I agreed.

"Online, on the "Just Ruthless" message boards, everyone is rooting for you two to get together." Hank added.

"You guys are so fucking lame." Adam continued to speak. "Chris, you're going to stay here with Redbone, I mean if you want."

Don't worry, there is more to the plan.

"Hell yeah, I want! There's no way that I'm going back home. Adam, it's been great. We'll need to chill sometime, but you need to go find Susan and I need to hang out here."

"Okay, tomorrow morning, Hank will take you, Adam, back home. Stay tonight and hang out with us, we have a little something, more low-key planned for the evening. We have all the episodes of "Just Ruthless" on TiVo, we'll hook it up to the projector in the ballroom and watch them. This way you can actually see what the whole world is going crazy over."

"How are they going crazy?" asked Adam.

"Man, they really sheltered you guys. I don't even know where to start. First of all, your faces are plastered everywhere. Well, except wherever you guys might be. The internet is full of websites discussing your lives, what you two will do next, if you're gay, if you're acting, if you and Susan will get together.

The craze isn't only here, but all over the world. People hate you guys so much, they can't help but watching you. Those who love you are getting themselves into all sorts of problems. People are telling off their bosses, their spouses, the police, and even random people on the street. It's insane."

"How badly do they hate us?" asked Chris.

"Let's just say that some of your shows leaked into a couple of Muslim conservative countries, many women saw how you guys interacted with Susan and how you let her talk back to you guys. Needless to say, some chick took off her ninja outfit, others followed and as a result a bunch of women got killed and now you guys have Jihads on your heads. But that's not all.

In China, you two have become an icon amongst the oppressed workers. There have been riots and protests leading to clashes between students, police and workers. They are following this "Just Ruthless" lifestyle. You two are a staple on all the news networks. Everyone is going nuts right now, asking where you guys disappeared to.

When you guys came here, they were just getting ready to start filming for the new episodes. Your bosses must be going insane right now. Adam, they're going to bug out when you go back without Chris."

"Bro, that might actually be lots of fun." Adam smiled as he said that and leaned back into the chair.

That night went as planned. Everyone gathered in the ballroom to watch the episodes of "The Rat Race" and "Just Ruthless". We paused it at times to ask Adam and Chris questions, but most of the time we would pause it to laugh at them or with them. Adam felt as if he was portrayed rather inaccurately. This bothered him a bit. Chris, on the other hand, loved it. He didn't care how bad they portrayed him to be; he felt that they were showing the world all the best parts of his life.

Isn't this exciting?

The skin at the end of Adam's penis had been cut off at birth, as were many of the skins at the end of many penises on American men of his age. This made Adam lose some sensitivity and an essential part of the male anatomy that he could of used to pass the time with more efficiently. Despite this missing portion of his appendage, Adam still had a very functional and eager penis. However, he had an angry penis. Being able to see is great, but imagine not having any eyelids. That's how Adam's penis felt.

The reason I tell you this is because on this particular morning, Adam, once again, woke up clutching to his manhood, as if it were trying to liberate itself from its border with his neighboring balls. The male penis is the most important thing in a man's life. The man who doesn't treat his penis well is a man whose priorities are misunderstood. Despite Adam's new found love and monogamous outlook towards life. His penis was still a sovereign nation and the constant stimulating bombardment caused by all the hot pieces of ass that had been surrounding him the past couple of days, has made his penis prepare for a coup d'etat.

He choked his penis like any dictator would on an opposing political figure. Then there came a knocking on the door. Adam's blood had been spending most of its time fighting in the Middle East; his penis curved that way. This made him slow to react to the knocking on the door.

Chris was lying in his bed. Sherry's black leg stuck out from underneath the sheets, her arm was draped over his chest. Chris's penis loved his leader. As a result, his blood was at rest and able to reach his mind much quicker. Chris looked over at Adam. Adam's eyes were open. Chris got out of bed taking the sheet with him, leaving a naked Sherry exposed. This infuriated Adam's penis even more. Chris looked down at Sherry and then over at Adam.

"I can't believe you're going to leave this place." Chris said as he opened the door to the room. It was Hank on the other side.

"Not only is he going to leave this place, but he gets to spend a couple of hours with me on the drive back." Hank grinned through his furry face.

Hank looks like a Hank. He was born with aviator glasses attached to his face and a white bushy goatee. His parent's were both black and stared at each other as the doctor pulled Hank's pale body out of his mother's womb. Hank was a product of genetic anomalies and chemical poisoning. His parents were very good, but very poor black folk. His father's pride and his mother's concern over the welfare of her future son forced the young couple to move out of their small apartment in Newark, New Jersey and into one of the only few houses that they could afford to buy.

The house was next to some oil refineries off route 1 and 9 in Elizabeth, NJ. They chose this house because it was the nicest one of all that they could afford. Obviously, there was a reason for the affordable price tag; although they were assured that living so close to such refineries were perfectly safe, someone obviously lied. Hank was born a white male with a white goatee and aviator glasses. I swear.

If it weren't for the glasses and the goatee, Hank's father would have quickly assumed the obvious. But since the entire situation was just so absurd, he did what many American black men of his age would do, he abandoned his wife and child and found a fat rich white woman to support him. Hank grew up to be a very confused black white man or white black man with a very powerful goatee and shiny glasses. All he ever wanted was a hug. Hank had the penis of an angry black man trapped in a white man's body.

By this point, Adam's penis had been defeated by the site of Hank. He sat up on his bed and looked up at Chris.

"Hey Hank, I'll meet up with you downstairs." Adam said to him.

"I'll be in Redbone's office. He'd like to talk to you before you leave."

"Alright."

Chris sat down on his bed, next to Sherry. Her perfect brown round ass served as a perfect spot for Chris to lay his right hand. He massaged it as he talked to Adam.

"Adam, it's been lots of fun but I'm glad you're leaving. You were beginning to annoy me with your damn arrogance and snotty attitude."

"Chris, shut the fuck up. Remember to follow the plan that Redbone gave us precisely. I'll see you soon. In the meantime, try not to have too much fun. Stick with Redbone and everything will turn out the way we want it to." Adam stood up and so did Chris. Chris went to shake Adam's hand but Adam continued to extend his hand past Chris and grabbed Sherry's ass.

"Sorry dude, I had to do that."

Chris shrugged his shoulders and lay down next to Sherry.

"Whatever man, I get to do a lot more than that." Chris smiled as he lay there.

Adam quickly got dressed and made it down to my office, but not before he made a pit-stop at the bathroom to shit, shave and shower. The three "sh" words that make any primordial beast into a respectable and happy man.

He entered my office. I sat at his chair behind the desk and Hank sat on the chair opposite of ME, on the other side of the desk.

"Adam, hello. Please sit down." I pointed with my open hand to an empty chair over to Hank's left. "Well, Adam. I hate to see you go, but your reason is a noble one and should therefore be respected by us all. This place is your home to come back to when ever you'd like. Our home and hearts are to be shared with you for as long as we are on this earth together. I hope you come back and visit. But Adam, just in case that we never see each other again, I'd like to thank you personally for sharing some of your time with me and with all of us. Take care." I came around the desk and shook Adam's hand. I then gave him a hug and whispered some final instructions into his ear.

"Hank take care of our good friend and take him home safely. And Hank, please hurry back, I've got some plans for the two of us tonight." I went back around to my desk chair and sat down. Hank and Adam both walked out of the room and out the front door. Outside stood a handful of the other house occupants. They were all there to bid a farewell to Adam; Big D was amongst them. Big D was more fragile than usual this morning. Most of the occupants of the house are usually still sleeping at this time in the morning, 9:30am, explaining the weak crowd.

Adam shook their hands, said his goodbyes and climbed into the van with Hank. Twenty minutes after they stepped out of the house, they were on the their way to take Adam back home. The ride was completely uneventful. Adam and Hank spoke for only ten seconds and this is how it went.

"Where'd you get those aviator glasses?" Asked Adam.

"None of your business." Replied hank.

Adam simply stared out the window, dozing on and off from time to time. Before he realized it, they were already back in the city.

Hank looked over at him and asked, "Am I taking you back to your place?"

"Take me back to the office, I want to see if Susan is there."

Hank said nothing; he simply kept on driving. A couple of minutes later he stopped the van. The office building's entrances were crowded with police. Remember, a lot of money is riding on Adam and Chris's return.

"Adam, you're going to have to get in the back of the van and hide under the seats. There's a blanket back there. Put it over yourself and I'll get us in through the service dock."

Adam did.

Hank drove up to the dock and spoke to the security guard; shortly after, they were driving right in. Hank told Adam to wait until it was clear for him to come out. Just as soon as Adam started to cramp up, Hank told him that it was okay for him to come out. Hank then brought him over to the service elevator.

"It's funny how they give some of us who work here access to everything." Hank said as he inserted a key into a keyhole next to the service elevator. He then pressed the up button and it opened up immediately. They both walked into the elevator. Inside, Hank had to insert his key into another keyhole in order to be able to operate the elevator. He pressed the button for Adam's floor.

Once again, Adam and Hank decided to spend their "quality time" by not speaking to each other. They didn't have to sit through too much silence before they reached the floor. The door flung open and the two men stepped out. Adam led the way towards Susan's cubicle. As they walked down the corridors, the heads of his ex-coworkers would pop out the tops or the sides of their cubicles, like prairie dogs. Before he reached Susan's cubicle, he stopped at his old, battered, cubicle. There was a man in a suit sitting down. On his suit was a badge, a shiny one, it definitely was much more impressive than the regular blue ribbons they pin on the other pigs in the county fair.

Adam walked over to Susan's Cubicle next. There was another man who must have won at the county fair. Adam stood there and looked at him for a moment, and then he turned around to look at Hank.

"Adam, don't you realize that you're special yet? You think only good things are going to keep falling into your lap? A lot of people are listening to you, a lot of them would do anything that you'd tell them to do and there are some people that I work for that worry when someone other than they can do that. Come on and follow me."

Hank lead the way back to the service elevator. Adam followed, the two prizewinners walked behind him. Adam slowed down a bit so that they'd be walking to his sides. The prairie dogs behind the cubicles continued to poke their heads out. Adam began to talk to the suits.

"Hey buddy nice shoes, I didn't know they came in asshole." He told the guy to his left. "I hear they make you guys squeeze lemons with your butt cheeks until you're just the right amount of stuck up." He told the guy to his right. They ignored him and continued towards the elevator, letting Adam lead the way. Once inside, Hank used his key to activate the elevator, he then pressed the top floor.

"You didn't think they would just give any worker here so much access did you?"

"Gee whiz Hank, very impressive. They gave you a bunch of keys. Did they give you those gay glasses too and is that goatee a privilege?" Adam grinned as he saw Hank cringe in anger. I told him all about Hank. He needed to know all the details. "I'm sorry Hank. What's the matter, daddy didn't love you?

Hank was really pissed off by the time that the elevator doors opened. He grabbed Adam and pushed him through the doors. On the other side was an office lounge, Hank grabbed him by the arm and lead him towards a door over to the left side of the receptionist's desk. Adam waived at the robust young receptionist as he was dragged by and through the door. She gave him a dirty look. Adam hadn't recognized the receptionist as the fat chick in the elevator.

On the other side was a large conference room with a large elliptical table in the center. There were twenty-five spots for people to sit at; only one was unoccupied. At the far end sat Pierre Nadaju. He yelled out to Adam to sit down at the empty seat. Adam couldn't hear him. Nadaju tried yelling for him to sit down again, but Adam just raised his hand ups in confusion.

"Sorry little man, you're going to have to talk a little louder. Try using a manlier pitch." Adam was able to yell this loud enough for everyone to hear.

"Sit the fuck down." Hank pushed Adam down on to the seat.

Nadaju decided to get closer to Adam. He walked down the right side of the table towards him. He told the man sitting next to Adam's right to move. The man did and Nadaju took his spot.

"Can you hear me now, asshole?" Nadaju didn't like to be upstaged in front of his peers; actually he didn't like to be upstaged in front of anyone at all.

"Sorry to embarrass you in front of your friends. Now get to the point where you tell me what you want me to do and how I have no choice." Adam responded.

"Well Adam, I'm going to be completely honest with you. You see, it's kind of the new fad, being honest. Everyone, everywhere is being honest, because of our little show, 'Just Ruthless', and frankly it's causing a lot of headaches. Now Adam, you have to understand that I am only the messenger here, but if we don't do anything to alleviate these headaches, we're going to be held responsible for all this and asked to pay.

The price that they want us to pay is not one that we're willing to pay. Therefore, you have to do a couple of things for us, for them."

"Where's Susan?" Asked Adam.

"Susan is fine. If you do what these men need you to do, everyone will be just fine."

"You bring me Susan and I'll do whatever you need me to do."

A man off to Nadaju's left stood up and began to speak. "You do what we require you to do and Susan will be released, unharmed."

"You don't bring me Susan now and I won't do what you require me to do."

"Adam, just do what we ask." Nadaju reached out and grabbed Adam's hand. He began to squeeze it tight with both hands.

"Adam, you don't want anything to happen to Susan, do you?" Said the man to the left.

"I don't care what you do to her or me, but I'll only help you if you bring her to me now."

Someone to the left, of the man to the left, whispered into the man to his right's ear, then the man to the left stood up once again. "Fine, it makes no difference to us as long as you do what we tell you. Bring the girl in."

A door to the far left opened up and Susan was brought in; she ran over to Adam. They hugged and embraced.

"Sorry for falling in love with you and getting you into this mess." Adam told Susan.

"Yeah, why'd you have to get all gay on me for?" Susan asked Adam.

"Sorry."

"Oh, and thanks a lot for telling them not to hurt me. You're a true gentleman." Susan said sarcastically.

Adam then motioned for Nadaju to move, so that Susan could sit next to him. Nadaju tried to get the man next to him to move, but the man refused. Nadaju was forced to stand.

"Okay, so what's the plan?"

"There are a couple of things that we need you to do Adam." Nadaju began to explain. "First of all, they want your friend Johnny Redbone. Hank over there has been undercover working hard for a couple of months to get enough evidence to be able to indict Redbone and everyone else in that house."

Before Nadaju could finish, the man to the left began to speak again, "They can do this the hard way or the easy way Adam; do you remember Waco or Ruby Ridge? Hank tells us they have drugs and weapons in there and says Johnny has shown them to you."

"I don't know what you're talking about, there aren't any drugs or weapons at the ranch."

"Oh shut the fuck up Adam, Johnny is always talking about the gardens and the weapons in the basement! I know you've been down there! I followed you two the other night!" Hank spat as he yelled at Adam.

"He never brought you down there?"

"He never trusted me enough."

"I guess daddy number two didn't love you either, so you stabbed him in the back." I had told Adam that night I took him down to the gardens that I suspected that Hank was a narc. I also told Adam about Hank's strange background. I knew Adam was going to use this information to his advantage. "How does it feel to have been born a wasted human?"

Hank grabbed Adam, but the man to the left told him to back off. Hank did.

"Adam, we want you to give us a tour of those gardens. We want you to get us Johnny Redbone and we want one more thing from you."

"What's that?"

"We need you to tell the world something for us. You see your little show is making a lot of people angry, and we're getting a lot of shit for it."

"Who is "we"? Who the fuck are you?" Asked Adam.

"My name is Tony Hevisac. I'm the network president. I've had to make a little deal with our friends at the federal government. I'll help them catch a notorious drug dealer and gun peddler and in return they won't fine me millions of dollars for all the damage 'Just Ruthless' has caused. They sent us Hank there to help us out. I know it sounds horrible, but there is very little else that we can do."

"And somehow you guys can make a couple of bucks off it too? I'm sure this will be a highly watched episode. 'Adam Stockton sells out!'" Adam added.

"Cheer up Adam. Why not make something tragic into something profitable?" said Mr. Hevisac.

"Well, It's what you guys do best, isn't it?" Asked Adam with a smile."

Mr. Hevisac laughed. "Why not? It's going to happen regardless, so why not make the best of it. This will be the last episode of 'Just Ruthless', broadcast live throughout the world. We will bring down some bad guys and bring peace to the world all at once."

"Bring peace?" Adam was a bit confused.

"The only way that we could have the government let us film all this is if we tell the world that it was all a show, that you are sorry for leading the world towards a great lie. You were acting upon selfish grounds and that 'Just Ruthless' is just a show, not to be taken seriously."

"So you need me to rat on some friends and lie to the world and then I can go free?"

"Essentially, that's what we're saying." Answered Hevisac.

"Let's do this." Adam stood up. He grabbed Susan's hand and pulled her towards him. He whispered in her ear, "Isn't this so exciting?"

Religion

Two vans left to go investigate the commune. Nadaju, Susan, Hevisac, Adam and Hank, who drove, were in one van and the camera crew was in the other. This time around, Adam seemed to have a lot more to say to Hank.

"Hank, do your black parent's know their son is a honky faggot? You want me to tell them? Hey Hank, I hear you've got your father's eyes. Hank are you technically a nigger? At least you weren't born a Jew, then your parents would have really hated you." Adam felt no need to hold back on Hank; he rightfully deserved a lashing.

Hank continued to drive without flinching, but you could tell by the sweat on his forehead and considering that the air conditioner was in full blast, that he was rather agitated. This made the trip feel much quicker this time around for Adam, but it must have been a living hell for Hank. I'm sure thoughts of driving off a bridge came across his mind.

The rest of the passengers were enjoying the trip and the banter. Despite the semi-seriousness of the pending situation, the atmosphere was pretty laidback. According to everyone, everything was going as planned, so there was no need to worry. If anything, it was a nice ride out to the countryside. They arrived to the ranch rather quickly. Adam's attacking of Hank sped up the trip in more than one way; aside from its entertainment value, it forced Hank to go well beyond the speed limit.

Once there, they all got out of the vans immediately. The camera crew quickly got all their equipment ready for filming. Adam was in reality not too comfortable with being in front of an actual camera. He didn't mind it so much when he couldn't see them, but being the central focus of a camera, and especially the mechanical man behind it, was rather unnerving to him.

"Alright, how do you want to do this? You want me to just walk right in, knock on the door? If you want, I can yell for them to come out. Maybe I'll throw some rocks through the windows and scare them out. Whatever is best for the camera." Adam said as he posed in front of the camera. He made all sorts of different poses, most of which he mocked from his childhood comic books.

"Adam, we're filming already! Just knock on the door!" Nadaju yelled to Adam.

"Oh. Okay well then, good evening America and everyone else. I'd like to welcome you all to the last episode of 'Just Ruthless'. Tonight will be a very eventful night with many surprises. There will be drama and maybe even some action. All of you might have been wondering where Chris and I have been for the past couple of days. I'm sure you all read some crazy rumors on the internet about how we might have moved up to Massachusetts and gotten married or kidnapped by terrorists for bringing western culture to goat fuckers, but you're wrong.

You see, the truth is that Chris and I have gone out and found Jesus. Yes America, by the name of our lord and savior Jesus Christ of Nazareth, son of God and Mary, Joseph's stepchild, and the only man to get nailed, come back as a friendly zombie and be praised for two thousand years. He has entered our hearts and our souls. We here at the Church of Immaculate Assumptions are a peaceful people. Please, let me show you the way."

Adam walked up to the front door and pressed the doorbell. The door opened quickly and on the other side stood Chris and Sherry, but not how you would expect them to be. Chris was clean-shaven and dressed in a shirt and tie. Sherry was also dressed pretty conservatively. She would give Ann Coulter a hard on. He let Adam and friends all in. The walls were adorned with religious paintings of Jesus and sheep, with his flocks of sheep. Baaaa. Sheep.

They all went into the ballroom where they disturbed a bible study group in mid session.

"Sorry to interrupt the class but we have some guests. Class please say hello to our guests. You already know Adam and Hank." Everyone began to introduce themselves to each other when Hank snapped. He grabbed a folding chair and launched it across the room.

"WHAT THE FUCK!!! This is bullshit. They're lying; they're all fucking lying. Where the fuck is Redbone? Fuck this shit! Show them the fucking gardens!" Hank yelled at Chris.

"Who is Redbone? Hank what's wrong with you, you know that the gardens are out back. You tend the tomatoes everyday yourself." Chris smiled at Hank with big doe eyes.

"You son of a bitch, I'm going to kill you." Before Hank could launch on top of Chris, some of the guys in the bible study group intercepted him."

"What the hell is going on here? I need some answers or else a lot of you are going to be royally fucked." Mr. Hevisac began to grow agitated. His plan was being ruined and with it his attitude.

"Take him to the walk-in freezer. Show him the basement!" Hank's glasses were sweating.

"Chris, we have to show them the basement. It's the only way out of this mess." Adam told Chris.

"Okay fine, if we HAVE to." Chris led the way out of the ballroom and into the kitchen. He opened the giant door to the walk in freezer; he pressed a button on the wall that exposed a keypad. Chris entered the combination and the door slid open. "Follow me."

Chris led the way into the basement. "As you can see the basement is full of supplies, food, clothes, water, all the essentials that a family like ours would need to ride out the apocalypse. We wanted to keep this a secret from all those who we didn't quite trust yet. Sorry Hank, that's why you never were brought down here. This is the livelihood of the entire family and now you've jeopardized our safety by bringing those cameras down here."

Nadaju quickly cut the cameras.

Hank was in awe. He didn't know how to react. The basement was set up entirely as a shelter. It was more than obvious what it was. I had a better plan than everyone else had. Not everyone in the ranch was a full-time resident. I had a lot of people on the road working for me. I hired Hank to be my delivery guy in Manhattan. In order not to look too suspicious, he took a job as a shipping and receiving clerk at the building the contained Hardmega Tech. The job would require him to be traveling around the city, so his deliveries would be inconspicuous. It was Hank who had brought up the idea to bring Adam and Chris to the ranch.

Now that I think about it, I doubt it was really his idea. I've known Hank for a while now and I've never known him to be ingenious, at all. I've got a feeling he got his position strictly due to his all around contribution towards affirmative action and the non-existing quota that affects our every day livelihoods. I was always a little weary about bringing new people to the ranch and I already had my doubts about Hank, so I decided to use this mess to my advantage.

Adam and I spoke of the plan to help us escape from the bullshit that was bothering us. I told Adam that I didn't trust Hank because I can't trust any man who can't look me directly in the eyes, regardless of the man's "condition", and in this case, especially because of the man's condition. I gambled on setting up Hank. At worst, Hank would have come back alone to the then now-Christian commune and it would have been played off as a joke. As for my disappearance, Hank would be getting a phone call any minute now. And as far as the things in the basement are concerned, you would be surprised how easy it is to get rid of a large amount of marijuana and an arsenal of guns and ammo. I know some guy named Chico.

Hank's phone rang. I thought it would take longer for him to call. Hank picked it up.

"Who the fuck is this?" Hank didn't recognize the phone number. I was calling from a rest stop, somewhere in Ohio.

I didn't answer Hank; I simply began to speak.

"When I was six years old I dreamt of getting the new He-Man 'Castle Greyskull' for Christmas. I wanted it so bad and I begged my parents and wrote letters to Santa. I stayed up at night ogling over a

Toys "R" Us catalog clipping that I had saved. Then that Christmas morning came along and I rushed to the shitty, tiny, white, tacky. little Christmas tree that we had. Under that tree awaited nothing but socks and underwear.

I was so disappointed. But, I didn't cry. It prepared me for an entire life of disappointments. Hank, life sucks. So don't cry. Don't be such a shady asshole and people would like you much more."

"REDBONE! You asshole! Where the fuck are you?" Hank yelled at the phone, but I had already hung up. "It was Redbone. He's fucking with me. He's fucking with all of us!"

"Hank, we'll let your bosses know how much you've helped us, but I think this is where we part. We did our part and you failed to deliver. So, this is where you and us are no longer associated with each other. Goodbye. Nadaju lets go. Let's rap this up." Said Hevisac.

"Okay Adam, this is where you look into the camera and tell the people what you need to tell them. Then we can rap this up and all be on our way. We'll fill the rest of the show with highlights. And we're recording in five, four, three and...." Nadaju signaled for Adam to speak.

"Well world, I have something to tell you all about this show, 'Just Ruthless'." Adam paused for a second and began to pace for a while. Nadaju motioned for him to speak. Adam stopped pacing and looked directly at the camera, he opened his mouth and...

"If your phone bill is too high, don't call so many people. If the price of gas is too high, don't use so much of it. If your bills are too high, don't spend more than you can afford. If your ass is too fat, stop eating so much shit and try exercising a little. But most importantly, this one comes right from the bottom of my heart to everyone out there. If you can't think for yourselves, go fuck yourselves. Just leave me the fuck alone.

Fuck 'Just Ruthless' and fuck you all."

"Cut!" Yelled Nadaju. "No! What the fuck is that?! Adam, try that again, but say the COMPLETE opposite. AND action!"

"About the show, about life and about all this," Adam then repeated what I had whispered into his ear the last time I saw him. "It's all bullshit." He then turned to Susan, grabbed her and gave her a long and sloppy kiss. When done, he looked back up to the camera and added. "Except that. The world needs more of that."

It was what everyone wanted to hear. Adam got to tell the truth. The truth being that everything really was bullshit. In order for Adam, Chris and I to escape from all the bullshit, we had to create our own bullshit. Bullshit had been piling up for so many years that our societal bodies have evolved to thrive off of it. If we don't provide enough bullshit then others will go into a bullshit-deficiency craze and attack all those who are slacking with their production. Nadaju and Hevisac ate the bullshit up and loved the happy ending.

Nadaju wrapped up the rest of the show as quickly as possible. He said something on the lines of, "Thank you for watching 'Just Ruthless'. The entire season would be available on DVD by the fall." Meanwhile, Hank had disappeared. He had taken one of the vans and set out to find me.

"Adam, I have something to tell you." Susan put her hand on Adam's cheek.

"Yes Susan?" Adam looked down at her.

"I don't love you."

"What?" Adam was a little shocked.

"You're kind of an asshole. Shit, you just assumed that I was in love with you."

"Well, everyone else kind of wanted us to hook up, too."

"And that's why I let you carry me along this entire stupid final episode. I figured I could go along with it and make a happy ending out of it. Regardless, since when do you care about what other people think?"

"I just thought, that we had something between the two of us."

At this time, Chris decided to interrupt the two and point out a slight problem.

"I hate to get in the middle of all this but your rides are gone. They all left. Hank took one van and the other pricks took the other one." Chris paused to think for a second. "I tell you what. You guys spend the night here, we'll throw one last party with all of us and you two can be on your ways tomorrow."

"This is like the fourth night in a row that I do this." Falsely complained Adam.

Susan tugged on Adam's shirt. He looked down at her.

"Just because I don't love you, doesn't mean that I don't care about you. It also doesn't mean that I don't want you to do whatever you want to me. Let's have fun tonight. Tomorrow there will be more time to talk." She said.

Adam decided to accept that request from Susan.

This Concludes Our Show

That night was the last night that Adam, Chris and Susan partied together. Adam and Susan both had their fun that evening with each other. They laughed, they danced, they had hot drunken sloppy sex and they slept in each other's arms. They would see each other a couple of more times after that night, but as a result of the show's popularity their lives were thrown into chaos. Susan went on the talk show circuit and had some fun with her fifteen minutes of fame. But as quickly as it came for her, it all went away. She now lives in Los Angeles, working as a producer for other reality shows.

On the way back from the ranch, Nadaju and the other guys in the van decided to stop at a rest stop. While Nadaju waited for the guys inside to purchase whatever snacks they wanted, he noticed some lights coming from the woods. He investigated further and found himself in the middle of a giant role-playing game battle. Nadaju might be a dick, but the man knows how to make money when he sees it. He introduced himself to the leader of the "Mighty Warrior Wizards of Watchung".

Six months later "Wizards and Warriors", Nadaju's new reality television show was another global phenomenon. The show sparked a reintroduction to medieval battles throughout Europe. During these days, "progressive power metal" ruled the world. This was the first show that Susan helped produce.

Joe A. Melendez

Adam disappeared. He couldn't deal with the fame for even a second. He cashed out as soon as possible and disappeared. There weren't many places in the world that he could disappear to without being recognized. Legend has it that he ended up in Tanzania for a while, until a couple of years later his show began to air there, too. I heard he opened up a bar on the Spanish Mediterranean. I hope he did.

Chris had fun. He had lots of fun. He and the rest of his roommates decided to sell the commune. A lot of them dispersed and did their own thing, but Chris and a few others decided to stick together and continue what Redbone had started. They now live in a Dutch farm somewhere in the Netherlands, doing whatever the fuck they want. Chris seems to still be having fun.

I did many things, too many for me to tell you all right now. I was destined to see and experience more things than any other man on Earth. As a result of this destiny, I was in this story. There are greater things to be discovered in this universe and my adventures will lead him to these things. Until he seizes to exist, he will continue to make his mark on all those that cross his path.

So there you go. That's it. The true story of Adam Stockton, Chris Gomez and everyone else who shared their experience with them, as they changed their world through ignorance and honesty on a stupid reality television show called "Just Ruthless". Let it be known that those two assholes are good people and the two coolest guys I've ever had the pleasure of meeting. Now, you'll have to excuse me. I have some business I need to take care of…

The End

Joe A. Melendez

www.ingramcontent.com/pod-product-compliance
Lightning Source LLC
Chambersburg PA
CBHW021012180626
46814CB00003B/1259